THE LAST AUTUMN

THE LAST AUTUMN

S.J. Newman

The Book Guild Ltd.
Sussex, England

This book is a work of fiction. The characters and situations in this story are imaginary. No resemblance is intended between these characters and any real persons, either living or dead.

This book is sold subject to the condition that it shall not, by way of trade or otherwise, be lent, re-sold, hired out, photocopied or held in any retrieval system or otherwise circulated without the publisher's prior consent in any form of binding or cover other than that in which this is published and without a similar condition including this condition being imposed on the subsequent purchaser.

The Book Guild Ltd.
25 High Street,
Lewes, Sussex

First published 1994
© S.J. Newman 1994
Set in Baskerville
Typesetting by Ashford Setting and Design Services
Ashford, Middlesex
Printed in Great Britain by
Antony Rowe Ltd.
Chippenham, Wiltshire.

A catalogue record for this book is available
from the British Library

ISBN 0 86332 900 4

To Caroline Sullivan

I

Miss Greycliffe dressed according to her name. She wore blue cardigans and white shirts, all of which matched her soft greyish-blue eyes and fair complexion and fair, long hair. She possessed a natural dignity, and walked in a way that displayed to unobtrusive perfection her fine figure, the mobility of feature and the flow of blood — quick, temperate, agile and clear. She blushed easily and naturally. You would not have known in talking to her whether it was the weather or the conversation which so stirred her, or whether the laughter lurking in her features was that of her *esprit de jeunesse* or had a more satirical meaning. At all events she was the picture of comely health and not more so than today.

Today she had been swimming, which she did with a languorous slow breast stroke, enjoying the sensation of the pellucid warm water flowing around her body. Now she walked in air and sunlight, down streets where silence itself swam after her, feeling still warm and as if embalmed in light, feeling the air eddy around her luxuriating form.

Life might be said to be good to Miss Greycliffe. Her work, as a psychiatrist, was adapted to her qualities of patience, good sense and tranquil ability to find the right words for difficult states of consciousness. She had unusual amounts of sympathy, some unobtrusive pity, and a kind heart. In many ways, despite the modern-sounding occupation, she was an old-fashioned person who believed in faith, common sense, and quiet practicality. Although she lived alone she was not lonely, yet she could understand the loneliness of weaker spirits who lacked her own capacities of endurance.

Her parents had died when she was young, leaving her with a brother only a year older who was a town architect — a job in which, unlike his sister, he struggled, finding that his desires for an old-fashioned, rather churchy architecture were not shared by his fellows, who looked for more modern and racy designs.

Nevertheless he subsisted, sending his sister comically petulant letters and cards to express his sense of unease in the world he tried to inhabit. She was very fond of her brother, felt he was younger, saw him whenever she could. He found her perplexingly invulnerable. In his heart, too, was glad that she was single to everybody except himself. He liked to imagine that he shielded her against the world.

They had lived thus, corresponding and sharing each other's company for some four years.

Elizabeth's serenity had indeed something shielded about it, but the shielding came from within. She was not apparently a shy person, yet deep down she was shy; though never obviously, with her brother. He called her Liz and teased her and she laughed, but with a strange vacancy as though some significance should have been found in the echoes and substratum of laughter to which she was blank. 'You are untouchable,' he said, and so she believed.

There was a reason for this untouchability, something which made her invaluable in her profession, where it was only too easy to make crude or overfamiliar errors in diagnosis. She communicated a mixture of firmness and shyness which was of enormous help to her patients, struggling often between an image of conformity and an intransigently helpless self that would not correspond to what ought to be. She never insisted. She knew how to touch with language, and the touch would often awaken baffled gratitudes and startled perceptions. Since she was unconscious of her powers she had no way, and neither had her patients, of registering these contacts, and as a result perfect confidence was established. It was second nature to her. She took her whole self to work without a thought of latent desires for privacy or the cost of making her privacy professional in this way. She spun innumerable private conversations out of her own resources in areas which were all too often professionally guarded. Where other doctors did research and recorded findings with slightly hysterical clinical exactitude, she was prepared to lose in the cause of finding. Nobody knew where they would be with Miss Greycliffe, neither did she.

The reason for this untouchability had to do with a latent sense of tragedy. Like the character in Hardy, 'she never expected much' — either for others or for herself. The death of her mother had left her strangely unwounded; her father's death had touched her more nearly. Where other doctors relied on some 'primal scene', both in themselves and in the patients — either that or an equally primal trauma, which they would dig into and if necessary invent — Miss Greycliffe had no such expectations. Her father had died in her sight; had fallen from a cliff on a family outing when she was quite young. Yet though the shock had made her faint she had no recollections of the scene. On coming to she remembered only clouds, massing grey and ice-bright in the west, and that sense of light climbing and falling from darkness was her enduring image of death, and so in a way of life. She was a mistress of displacement.

It was strange that her mother's death had meant less. From her mother she derived all her strength and latent nobility of character, from her father an equally latent cynicism. Her mother's life had been one of moral and emotional hardship, of finding her ideals battered and untreasured, and mainly surviving through opposition. Yet it was the father she remembered. 'Never marry, Lizzie,' he had teased her, 'all life is selfish at heart, you'll find.' She had never found it so, but she had never inquired into the nature of selfishness closely. She supposed it must be so for he had told her so, but she put away the thought with the advent of each new patient.

Today, however, she was on holiday. A letter of comic perplexity from her brother had suggested a trip to the seaside — to a little town under steep crumbly chalk cliffs, with a fishing harbour, where they would stay in a guest house and walk and talk, and watch the swimmers. Nigel could swim but preferred to stay on shore, laughing at her as she bounced among the waves in her orange bathing cap, until she grew reserved and sat with him on the beach, listening to the radios and the queer squeaky voices of children. Nigel had hired deckchairs, which scrunched at uneven angles amid the pebbles or sank awkwardly into the sand. She was sitting now with her skirts kirtled over her knees, feeling the cool air and hearing the yarking scream of gulls. Once, as the afternoon wore on, a heron flew heavily overhead, its legs golden in the setting sun, for it was late summer, and the beach was dark by eight o'clock, leaving only the flashing of harbour lights and the pattern of light from fish shops and restaurants.

'There's a man at my office, Liz' began Nigel and stopped.

She laughed. 'Only one?'

'He's younger than me, not by very much. He makes you think.'

He thought for a moment, wrinkling his somewhat unwrinkled brow.

She had been humming music to herself; the conversation fell into awkward turns of her brother's inarticulacy.

'He does all sorts of things.'

'So do you.' She reassured him. He was like a younger brother, often seeking consolation.

'We get along very well. I think.'

'You think.'

'He knows more than me. But we have similar ideas.'

A boat came in, laden with trippers, a little steamship with gaily painted lifebuoys. The shingle churned as the people got off.

'Shall we go for a ride?'

'He does say interesting things. He's got an active mind.'

They watched the boat loading again. A funny old salt in a sou'wester, pulling at his pipe, took the fares.

'It would be fun.'

'I asked him down for a day.'

'Where?'

'Here.'

'Oh Nigel ...' She looked at him quizzically. 'I bore you, don't I?'

He pooh-poohed the suggestion, but looked anxious. 'Don't ever say that, Liz. You keep me sane. Lizzie.'

He didn't often used his father's diminutive. She touched his hand reassuringly.

'He makes me think about all sorts of things. He's — he's sort of sublime.'

She said nothing. The boat pulled away. Waves flopped on the shore like sea lions.

'I can't work out if he's very lazy or very patient. Work gets done around him, but he never seems to enjoy it very much. He knows more about architecture than anyone in the office but nobody listens to him.'

'Except you.'

'I think he has genius, but he doesn't know what to do with it.'

She paused. 'But you listen to him. That's probably the best thing. Brood, drift and obey.'

He looked up startled. 'That's right.'

'It's a writer.'

'He writes a bit. He has ideas. I think he gets very depressed. But it's hard to tell. He's a very laconic chap. When things go wrong, he just says, "Ah well". But I can see he's disappointed.'

'You know what Father said. Nobody's satisfied in this life.'

'Mother said it isn't the thought that counts, it's what you make of it. And I can't see him making anything. He's frustrated somehow. I get the impression that he's like a radio off-station. Messages go to and from his mind but most people can't unscramble them. He's waiting for something.'

'He must be lonely.'

'I'm not sure. Liz, he's a bit of a ladies' man.'

She laughed again. 'Is that why you invited him?'

'He says women are somehow mixed up with his dreams of whatever it is.'

'Nigel, I'm off duty.'

'I know you are, pet.' He was anxious to reassure her and very cumbersome. She took his hand.

'There's another boat.'

'All right.' They stood up, went across to the shore. The boat was tossing on the waves. A group of trippers climbed aboard laughing.

'Shall we?'

'All right.'

The boat tossed beside a concrete mole. Nigel and the captain handed her down respectfully, and she was seated in the stern, smelling the smell of fresh paint and salt. Nigel was fitfully gay, startling the other passengers with snatches of sea shanty. Once he broke into Stanford's 'Drake is in his hammock' and made everybody laugh. Elizabeth did not mind. She loved his moods, found them strangely restful. Once he took her hand, dallying with it like a lover.

'He thinks a building should be like a sea shell, full of strange internal harmonies.'

'Who — oh your friend.' But the phrase settled into her mind.

'He builds organs, you know, and plays them. Even though he says it spoils the touch for the piano.'

'Nigel dear, I'm sure I shall like him very much.'

The boat dipped and rocked. They went round by the North Foreland, and landed on a rocky beach.

'No more than half an hour, ladies and gents, otherwise tide'll turn,' warned the skipper.

The foreshore was an entrancing place, under big cliffs the colour of old newspaper, full of rock pools where miniature marine life frisked and flittered in the shadows. At first they walked with the captain, who jerked his pipe stem towards the yellow mass of the Goodwin sands. 'Many a fine ship them sands has swallered,' he volunteered. Later they walked alone.

Nigel found a cliff path and insisted on climbing it.

'Don't,' she warned, for it looked dangerous, but he was already gone, skipping from boulder to boulder like a mountain goat. Reluctantly she turned away, and explored the caves and pools with their fluctuating brown seaweed. She got down on her knees and gazed into the shallow lakes, her breath close enough to stir the surface. She caught glimpses of her face, surrounded with hair that flared grey in the watery light; it looked pale and aloof, shadowily stirred by the play of ripples. The tide was far out, and the only sound was the flutter of a breeze across the pools. There were one or two little fishing boats stranded out there where the sea, like a band of silver, nibbled at the edge of the sands, and she could see the specks of fishermen moving about on the greyish-yellow surface. All the other trippers seemed to have disappeared.

She stayed still among the rock-pools until her ears warned her that a change was coming. Very far off she could hear the rush and roar of the tide. A bell was ringing. The fishermen had disappeared. The band of silver was significantly wider. There was no sign of her brother.

She was in a dilemma. If she stayed the tide would come in and she would have to climb the cliff path. If she went to the boat the captain would embark immediately. She could hear shouts.

She turned towards the boat. It was already evening. A great golden sun loomed out of the sea with high clouds around it. Seabirds were flocking and calling to each other. The air itself had changed and breathed wetness against the cliffs. Tiny rivulets of the incoming tide were already apparent in the rock pools, which looked agitated and cloudy rather than crystalline.

She reached the boat. There was a board up which she had to walk, for the narrow channel was filling, and the boat heaved on the incoming waves.

'Now then, missee,' said the boatman, 'keeping us all waiting, aren't yer?'

'I'm sorry.' She found herself fumbling for apologies. 'My brother.' She looked back. Striations of sunlight grooved patterns in the chalk-face, giving it a strange scooped appearance like a disused quarry. 'My brother's climbed the cliffpath.'

'More fool he,' said one of the trippers heartlessly. Elizabeth looked at him in desperation.

'Is it dangerous?'

'Dangerous!' It was the captain laughing. 'He'll take no harm up there. Them cliffpaths go miles inland. They ent steep. We wouldn' take a boat hereabouts if there was no danger. A difficult chalky climb, but he'll be inland by now, out o' harms way. Fine bracing walk on the land'ard side, and he'll be back by supper, rarin' to go.'

Elizabeth looked back once again.

'Now missee,' warned the skipper. 'Time and tide, you know. (Young lady's lost her young man in them cliff paths,' he added parenthetically to the other voyagers.)

There was a chorus of protest. One fat lady complained about keeping her husband waiting.

'Wait just a moment,' beseeched Elizabeth. She was blushing and furious at herself for doing so. She wanted to explain that Nigel wasn't her young man. She looked back again and was convinced she saw a head bobbing about on the cliffpath. There was a faint cry.

'Oh,' she insisted, 'it *is* him. Please wait!'

There was a brief stir and an argument among the passengers. The tide was coming in fast now, and the water around the boat was choppy. The rock pools were rapidly turning into lakes and the caves into watery grottoes. Already the paths to the boat were filling up, becoming impossible.

'Better not to wait,' warned the skipper.

'Oh *please*!' cried Elizabeth. She turned back in anxiety, waved, slipped and turned her ankle nastily among the rocks.

'Oh!' she cried again, in vexation and pain, feeling herself to be a comical and absurd sight, tumbling around among rock and water. A wave broke nastily, drenching her stockings; she caught her skirt up above the knee, feeling a fool. She tried to inch forward towards the boat, biting her lip, blushing and angry with herself. If only time would stand still a moment! The boatman was extending an arm, laughing pacifically. She wouldn't take it, but inched forward towards the plank. It was wet and slippery. Her ankle hurt abominably. She could hear crunching footsteps on the foreshore behind her, a man calling her name, but she could not look back. There was something odd in the call but the confusion of the moment was upon her and she was concentrating on two inches of plank at a time.

'No, please don't touch me,' she gasped at the captain, inching further, holding her lip between her teeth almost until it bled, looking down with intense concentration at her black sandy shoes. She could see the water heave, feel the boat move with the waves, was dizzy with the effort of concentration. It was such a tiny distance to cover.

There was splashing behind her, strong masculine footsteps beating through water; in an instant she felt an arm round her waist. She cried out, but the arm guided her forcibly into the boat. She collapsed on a seat near the stern, half crying, wanting to laugh, with a mixture of tears and brine stinging her face.

'It's so absurd.'

She was apologising to everybody, to the skipper who was laughing stoically above her as he guided the boat through the channel, to the other passengers, to her brother who was still holding her as she let her eyes crawl over the unfamiliar garments, up towards the unfamiliar bearded face. 'Oh, Nigel,' she said at the very moment she realised it was not her brother.

He raised his hat without relinquishing his hold of her. 'Rex,' he said, 'Rex Buckley.' She recognised him in an instant. It was the name of her brother's friend.

'Tiddn't 'xactly the one she left wi'', observed the captain, as if to a gathered assembly, and there was laughter in the boat as the tension relaxed.

Elizabeth looked down again in confusion; her hair fell about her face.

'Oh, Mr Buckley,' she beseeched, 'where is Nigel?'

'We met among the rocks. He was hurrying on and had slipped and slightly hurt his leg. I said I would go to the boat and let you know. He's all right. There's a bus stop in the lane. He'll be in Eastminster before us. I never intended to meet you in this way. If the tide hadn't been running so fast

I'd have returned the way I came, but there was no time.' As he spoke he withdrew his arm, but reluctantly. She was still confused. 'He's hurt ...?'

'Nothing to mention, he turned his ankle on the rocks. He's perfectly all right.'

'It seems such a strange coincidence, you being there ...'

'I was walking. It's the obvious road out of Eastminster. A lovely lane full of fuchsias until you come to the chalk. Look, I've been blackberrying.'

He pulled a handkerchief out of his pocket. It was stained dark with the fruit. He took several and, before she knew what was happening, he had placed them between her lips. Her mouth opened and closed on the gritty texture, feeling the juice burst into her mouth. She could feel herself blushing again through a tumble of hair. Her eyes made the light sparkle strangely.

They bounced across the waves with the light darkening around them. The lights of the town were already reflected on the water. They slipped in between the harbour lights, into the stiller, silken, oily water of the harbour. The tide tapped against the sides of the fishing boats and slapped the sides of the mole. The trippers clambered ashore. Rex tipped the boatman; he saluted and extended an arm to Elizabeth. She took it gratefully, feeling a voltage of pain through her ankle. She gasped, winked back the tears. Her face was very white.

Rex was by her side, supporting her. 'You too?' he said. She nodded, gasped on a laugh.

'We're a very close family.'

He supported her up the beach, compelled to walk at her speed, and evidently enjoying his burden. She felt her breasts swing heavily against his shirt, but was unable to support herself properly. She felt helpless in his arm, like a child, helpless and almost sick with hurt. They made a slow progress towards their boarding house, which was on the front. He almost carried her up the steps and over the threshold. There, sitting in a chair in the hall was her brother. He too looked pale.

'Liz. Rex. You found her. You told her.'

'Those confounded rocks. Liz, I was following a butterfly and I slipped ... Ridiculous. I had to hobble to the bus.'

'Watch out,' warned Rex, 'I think she's fainting.'

She was in a very strange state. Weakly she felt them helping her up the stairs to her room, saw them turn on the lights, felt her brother's arms tenderly around her as they laid her on the bed. She sobbed once, and was asleep immediately.

II

The following day they met at lunch. There were proper introductions and plans for the remainder of the holiday. All night she had lain in her strange state, not properly sleeping, not properly waking, her leg aching, and her mind and body moved between the voice and feel of her brother and those of his friend. He had touched her! She thrilled all through at the remembered sensation.

To meet again was an embarrassment. Mr Buckley was cordial. She felt baffled. Too much had happened. She could not forget that he had touched her. Covertly she looked at the hands on the table-cloth. They were strong and simple and pouched — that was how she thought of them — *pouched*, with black hair on the wrists and behind the knuckles.

Mr Buckley thought of her too; thought of the light weight of her as he lifted her into the boat, and later of the walk up the beach. He looked her full in the face and was sad to see the shadows under her eyes. He enquired about her ankle. She laughed nervously.

Nigel watched astounded. His sister was never nervous. Always capable, practical, rock-solid in conversation; and now — on edge, she seemed. It must be the fall. He himself felt shaky and baffled. Something seemed to be happening that disturbed simplicities. He looked at his sister again. She was blushing. Well, she often did that. It was part of her shyness. But he did expect her to take more interest in his friend, to ask questions, to follow the leads he had given. Somehow he expected her to help Rex. Circumstances could not have turned out better, after all. All the silly bits of meetings — introductions — over in a flash. They were already friends last night. She was laughing to him in her very special way. But now everything was on edge.

Rex himself seemed baffled, searching for the right thing to say. Everything felt wrong. It was like squinting into a broken kaleidoscope.

He rooted among fragments of conversation like a diligent archaeologist with a small portion of what might prove to be a rare find. But his interventions only made things worse. The pieces scattered, would not interlock.

Eventually he had a flash of inspiration.

'We can't walk anywhere, but we can row; at least Rex and I could.'

This was a wonderful idea. Rex left immediately and returned in half an hour with the news that he had managed to find a boat by the harbour, if they could get there: the best thing to do was to ring for a taxi; in fact he had done this already. They arrived at the harbour to find the boat waiting for them. It was arranged that Rex and Nigel should each take an oar and Elizabeth should sit in the stern, holding the tiller-ropes. After a very little while only Rex was rowing and the two invalids were taking it in turns to steer. There was much amusement at the beads of sweat that broke out on Rex's face.

Eventually Nigel said, 'It's wrong. I wanted you two to talk. With two lame ducks in the boat we seem only able to make a nuisance of ourselves. Rex, I want you to put me out.'

'Here?' teased Rex, rocking the boat stealthily. Elizabeth laughed, naturally again.

'He was the only one not to get wet yesterday.'

'On that spit of beach.'

'Suppose the tide comes in again.'

'You'll have to rescue me.'

'Like Edie Ochiltree,' said Elizabeth.

'Who?' said Nigel.

'He's a character in Scott. He saved people when the tide came in. Heroically.'

'Oh. Well, you don't have to be heroic, but I shall want saving.'

They landed him as he requested, and left him there, sitting alone and forlorn amidst the shingle.

'Mr Buckley,' said Elizabeth, resuming the tiller.

'Rex,' he replied.

'We scarcely know each other.'

'But better than many people who think they do.'

'Yes.' She pondered. 'Nigel told me about you.'
'Did he?' He said lightly enough.
'Does that sound inquisitive? I never asked.'
'What did he say?'
'He said you thought buildings should be like shells.'
'Did he?' It was his turn to ponder. 'Miss Greycliffe.'
'Elizabeth.'
'Yes. You know about people.'
'My work ...'
'Yes. Are they happy?'
'*Happy*? I scarcely expect ... They have problems.' She thought of the sad ashen faces of her patients, the stories, the voices, the hallucinations.
'They scarcely know who they are.'
'Are they old?'
'Mainly. Some are young.'
'Idiots?'
'Sorry?'
'Sorry. I meant not in the morbid sense. People whose lives are hidden with God.'
'Sometimes. Weird sublimities mixed with weirder cunning. Sometimes on the verge of epilepsy ...'
'Sheets of light.'
'Yes.'
'Looking out of the water. What do you see?'
She looked. It was afternoon again. The tripper boats were plying. The beach was full and colourful, with striped awnings and umbrellas and sandy bodies. On the promenade people were strolling. The shops were crowded. You could see electrically red tin buckets and spades, and, tracing lines among the beach and the chalets you could see armies of children at work building fortresses and canals.
'People.'
'So do I.
She laughed.
'Do you know your people?'
She darkened. 'Scarcely.'
'They come to you for help.'
'Yes.'
'Do you choose them?'
'I ... select them. Some are selected for me.'

'You help them.'

'I, yes, up to a point.'

'At what point do you cease to help?'

A more professional person than Elizabeth would have been able to answer this question. She found herself blushing again as she answered.

'I scarcely know. I think I know what you mean. Are they mended or only prevented from marring themselves further?'

'Partly that. How far do you concern yourself with their *being*; afterwards?'

She scarcely knew. Her steering had grown erratic. She had become mesmerised both with the sound of his deep voice and with the way he pulled on the oars, leaning forward inquisitorially, his eyes seeming to burn into her face. To look directly at him was confusing; she liked to turn away slightly, but in so doing lost her sense of where they were going.

'You've steered us in almost a circle.'

'Yes. How foolish of me.'

He was looking at her tenderly and very closely. She took the tiller again with a certain truculence

'I *will* steer us straight. I was concentrating on other things.'

'So many people.'

'Yes.'

'We know so little.'

'You?'

'I have to build them houses. Tin boxes. How can you put dreams in boxes?'

'You can dream anywhere.'

'I doubt it. Elizabeth what I mean is . . .'

'Yes . . .' When he called her by name she felt a mixture of terror and excitement. She bit her lip.

'People are coffins.'

'Absurd.' Some indignation was working inside her now.

'We plan and build. Open style. Precincts. Holiday camps. All a kind of prison camp. People are supposed to be happy. What a mean idea.'

'Yes.' She felt very vague, wanted him firmer.

'We are supposed to know people.'

'What people want they generally get.'

'Do you believe that?'

'No.'

'Neither do I. How can you *know* people?'

'I don't understand. There's no such thing as a knowable person.'

'How can you feel with people? Know their wants, their needs, their inner language, their dialect of emotions.'

'A telephone dial presented itself to her mind. She laughed, feeling flippant, was ashamed, quickly.

'I have an aunt. She lives in a big house. People think she's mad. She has servants.'

'I don't think I understand.'

'I try to expand people's hearts and minds. But I scarcely know how ... Elizabeth, will you be my wife?'

This was so entirely unexpected that she took her hands off the tiller altogether. The boat drifted with the waves. Hardly knowing what she was doing, she dipped her arms in the water, feeling its delicious coldness slide off her.

'You will help me to reach people.'

'How?' It was like the proposal of St John Rivers. She felt abandoned and unhappy. 'I scarcely know you.'

'I know you. Elizabeth, I love you.'

The conversation had gone absurd. If only he had not said that. The words were so crude, they unsettled all her more complex reveries.

'I withdraw that question.'

'I hardly know what to say.'

'You do like me, Elizabeth, don't you?'

'Yes.'

'He seized her hand. 'I love you.'

'It's ridiculous. People don't.'

'People.' He was teasing, mocking, sardonic. Suddenly she was with another man. The first had made her feel worldly by being unworldly. This one made her feel unworldly by being worldly.

'Look at all those people over there. To them we're like them: two specks in a boat.'

'A boat that is being driven very erratically. Rex, I must have two hands for the tiller.'

He relented, but his hand brushed her skirt and petticoat as he took it away, and she felt the brush with a great shock through her body. It has been said that a woman's clothes are only an extension of the body. For the first time in her life Elizabeth felt physical, embodied, all sensation. Under her clothing her skin was taut with excitement.

'You are all woman, you know.'

In her confusion this still seemed an absurd thing to say for at the moment she felt part like a man . Her blue eyes kindled.

'If I were a man I should knock your block off.'

'You have strange powers ...'

'I have some real ones.' But she didn't want to lose him. He was aflame with her beauty. After a short struggle she found he was sitting in the stern with her.

'Elizabeth, look at me.'

She looked, and he saw her eyes fastened reluctantly on his, shrouded with dark lashes.

'I can't help it Elizabeth, I'm going to kiss you. I wanted to ever since — ever since ...'

'Yesterday.' The word was prosaic but the feeling behind it was emphatically not. He took her face to his; she felt the warmth stirring the hair of her neck, and rousing the curls from their slumber. She wanted to turn but was hypnotised by his brown earnest eyes. Tremblingly she touched his hand.

'Rex ...'

'Say it, my dearest.'

'Rex, when you touched me yesterday ...'

'I know, I felt it. Oh, Elizabeth, say you will!'

'No I cannot, Rex, do not bully me,' she said, but the no was long-drawn and reluctant and the other words were quickly buried by his fervour.

There was a long silence, broken only by the chopping and clatter of waves against the boat.

'We've drifted ever so far,' she said eventually.

'Elizabeth, listen. "In the second century of the Christian era the empire of Rome comprehended the fairest part of the earth and the most civilised portion of mankind." '

'What is it?' she asked, moved by the weird beauty of the sentence.

'It's the beginning of Gibbon's *Decline and Fall of the Roman Empire*. Life in a state of suspended contentment. Not for nearly a hundred pages do we learn that this long peace and uniform government of the Romans introduced slow and secret poison into the vitals of the empire.'

'Are you quoting again?'

'Yes.'

'It sounds terrifying.'

'Elizabeth, we are the Romans again. All this peace.' He buried his face in her lap a moment. Awkwardly she stroked his hair.

'What about the poison?'

'Barbarism and Christianity.'

She laughed. 'Nature and love, you mean. Are you either?'

'No. I'm not sure. Are you a Christian?'

'Not exactly.'

'What are you? Don't answer. You're a pagan divinity.'

'If I am I'm a faded goddess.'

'Helen.'

'Elizabeth.'

'Yes. I'm a fool. A fool of fortune. With you . . .' He stopped. 'It isn't easy. It won't be easy. Elizabeth I'm going to ask something difficult of you.'

'What?'

'Leave your practice.'

'Just like that? It's impossible.'

'I said it would be difficult.' He wasn't really talking to her now, he was muttering. 'There's another hitch.'

'What is it?'

'I can't tell you.'

She was utterly baffled. Desultorily she took the tiller, tried to make the boat go straight, failed. Not essentially an articulate person, but one who made do from day to day, she found the idea of a map, any kind of map, alien and alarming. Besides there was the sense of risk. At the hospital she worked as part of a team, like the viola in an orchestra — low-voiced but indispensible. And then there was the problem of money. She was not rich. Her parents had not provided for her. It would be hard to leave a territory where she felt to some extent protected and move away on her own. Anyway, what exactly was he asking? He wanted her to leave and live with an aunt. Would he be there? What kind of woman was she? It was all so nebulous. The shock of love had subsided; now they were like Robinson Crusoe and Man Friday, struggling to make sense of unfamiliar territory. She thought of her brother and looked for him. He too was a speck on a gravel strip. She needed him suddenly, desperately.

'Mr Buckley — Rex — will you row again?'

He left her side reluctantly, and took the oars. As he began to row articulacy returned and he began to explain.

'She lives alone. In a big house. I shouldn't be there, of course. I think she needs help. She's not very sane, you know. She keeps servants. She thinks she belongs to another century. She needs — I can't explain this properly — she needs a maid.'

'A maid?'

'A lady's maid. To let down her hair, dress her, and so forth.'

'Does she? They must be very hard to find.'

'Darling Elizabeth, she needs you.'

'Me? As a lady's maid?'

'I told you it wouldn't be easy.'

He explained further. He told her that his aunt was old, ill, wrong in the head, imagined that the past was still alive, and needed patience, care and constant attention.

'I want you to stay with her and win her confidence,' he said. There's another thing too. She thinks I'm a fortune-hunter and she's banned me from the house. I shan't be able to visit you. But I'll write.'

Elizabeth was baffled beyond belief, but an idea began to form in her head. A pledge, a challenge, even — to the spirit of farce that lurked within her — a lark. She listened again.

'How long does your holiday last?'

She told him.

'You could try for that time.'

She began to feel cross, petulant, at odds with herself and everybody.

'It was supposed to be a holiday. What will my brother think?'

'I've asked him. He says you'll do it.'

'Give up everything and help the rich.'

He hadn't expected the sarcasm.

'She isn't rich, well she is. But she's poor, she's mad. Elizabeth, she's a piece of old England which I'm trying to save. I need someone sympathetic, someone who will understand. She'll bully you frightfully. I promise you, you will feel very poor.'

This wasn't what she had intended either. 'You make me feel wrong, whatever I say.'

He looked at her with a weird kind of triumph.

'Does that mean you'll do it?'

'I expect so.' She felt exhausted. The pain had returned. 'Rex, please take me home.' She set her mind to steering a straight course.

They arrived at the spit of shingle. Nigel welcomed them jubilantly.

'I watched you all the way. Liz, you're a terrible navigator, you were all over the place. What did you lose?'

'Lose?'

'I saw you huddled in the stern. Don't tell me you didn't lose something. Rex, she's always losing things. She'd lose her head if I weren't there to make sure it's fixed on properly.'

'Her handbag fell off the seat,' said Rex, 'we had to pick everything up.'

'I knew it! Just like yesterday! Don't get me wrong, Rex, she's as wonderful as I told you, but only as long as she's in control.'

He mocked her until he saw her looking white and perplexed. Then he became solicitous. 'I've a wonderful idea!'

'No more wonderful ideas for me today,' laughed Elizabeth. 'I'm very tired.'

'Yes of course, Lizzie, but listen, it's for tomorrow. There's a cricket match, I read about it in the paper. There's a lovely ground on the cliff tops. We can go and sit in the sun and talk and applaud. It'll be like old times, when I was little, do you remember? I was always going to be a great cricketer, Rex, when I wasn't going to be a great singer or a great violinist or a great architect. Liz will tell you all about it. She's a great spectator and always has been. She knows much more about it than I do. She used to make tea for us when I was a boy. She knows all the positions, and exactly why they change bowlers, and whether it was a dropped catch or only a near miss.'

'I'm sure Miss Greycliffe is ...'

'No, you're not sure Miss Greycliffe is anything,' said Elizabeth firmly. 'Nigel, we would love to go, all of us, and tomorrow I will tell you something even more surprising than the kind of trousers silly mid-off is wearing, for Mr Buckley — Rex, I call him, has a plan which will interest you nearly as much as it has interested me.'

'You've told her Rex, by Jove,' said Nigel.

'Yes, I've told her.'

Nigel whistled. 'And did she say ...?'

'Yes,' said Elizabeth, looking at Rex, 'she said yes.'

Nigel whistled again. 'I knew she would,' he said. 'She was always streets ahead of me in those kinds of things. A natural winner in a way.'

'Even though she keeps losing things?'

'Liz, you know what I mean. I told you she would, Rex.'

It seemed natural for Mr Buckley to take her arm as they went to the taxi, and to engage her in conversation a moment at the door of the boarding house. Nigel hobbled indoors, but they stood a moment in the street with the fragrant smells of sea air, cliff grass and restaurants around them. They were both reluctant to part. She could not believe, still, that it was anything more than a game of make-believe to give spice to their love. He paced up and down several times pensively with his hands in his trouser pockets, and she stood looking at him with her lips parted. Neither had forgotten the feel of their bodies in the boat. Eventually he turned to go. She took his arm for a moment, walked a little, said she felt better. He turned down his full face on her upturned one and kissed her. For a moment they were in each others' arms. Then she went indoors.

She went up to her room, tense with conflicting emotions of love, bafflement and hostility. As she pulled down the blind she seemed to see his dark form in the street. She felt exhausted, but too excited to sleep. She slipped out of the room and hobbled down-stairs, ignoring her ankle. It was much better anyway.

She went out into the street. There was no sign of him. Crowds were strolling along the promenade. Children were carrying balloons and fish and chip suppers. The air was stirring and alive. Far off towards the pier there were lights and music. The tide was nearly in, reminding her of yesterday, the waves crashing on the shingle. Far out to sea there were the misty lights of ships in the offing. She walked a little among the crowds, and found him there, with his back to her, sitting on a bench. She stood behind him uncertainly. He was saying her name over and over again. She wanted to touch him, but eventually decided not to, and moved away into the crowd. Later she wished she had stayed with him.

III

She stood on the platform, watching the receding train. The white steam curled above the few bushes that hid the curve of the line, evaporating in the pale evening. A moment more and the last carriage would pass out of sight, the white gates of the crossing swinging slowly forward to let through the impatient passengers.

An oblong box painted reddish brown and tied with a rope lay on the seat beside her. A man came up to her and saluted. He wore a rough cut leather and tweed suit and had a red face with a ginger moustache.

'Miss Greycliffe?'

'Yes.'

'Surtees, ma'am. The car's in the forecourt. Carry your box.'

'Thank you.'

'T'aint above two mile to the house, but no cause fer walking, my lady says.'

'Thank you.'

'Dingle railway's nice to watch, slow to travel on. But better'n them smelly diesel cars.'

'Yes.'

'See yer brought a box. Nice n' handy. I'll collar it for you.'

He collared it and carried it heavily to the waiting car; a big black limousine. She sat in the back and he reported places on the drive that they had passed.

'That's Hudson's farm. Nice fresh milk we collect daily from there. See the old castle. My lady's arms come from there. Rights o' conquest. She's a tartar, the old 'un. Reg'lar has us in crotchets. But you'll find out. Familiar wi' the ropes?'

'The ropes. Of the box?'

'Of the job. She won't bide no messin'.'

'Not very familiar, I'm afraid.'

'T'ain't no lark,' he warned her. 'Miss Oldcastle don't stand fer much. Many a maid's bin lost to her through careless ways. Ain't in love or nothin' like, pardon my askin'.'

'No.'

'Just as well. Last one's a proper hoyden. Left lookin' big as a milk churn, an' wi' no references fro' Miss Oldcastle. Choose how, that's no way fer to carry on in our house, she says. Not but there ain't a bit er carryin' on now and then when wind's fro' southerd.'

He turned round in his seat and winked. 'Me n' Miss Bessie. Not to mention Ron.'

'Ron.'

'The butler. E's a one. Steer clear o' him an' you'll come to no 'arm. Miss 'All, she's the 'ousekeeper.'

'Miss All?'

'Not All. 'All. She's a stickler. You'll meet 'er first. Over tea. Outline yer duties.'

It all seemed as if prepackaged. She had agreed with Rex at least to try the job for the remainder of the holiday; they had spent a day at the cricket match and another day making preparations. And now this. She was dropped into another world of servants and badinage. Was she supposed to be a doctor or a patient? How would she cope with her duties? Would Miss Oldcastle detect that she was not a true lady's maid, and if so, would she mind? Elizabeth suspected that she would mind, very much. Was it all a game? Perhaps Miss Oldcastle was simply a rather batty old-fashioned lady. Or perhaps it was all some complex love tryst devised by Rex. She would find out.

Meanwhile they were passing through a large park with cattle browsing under sunlit trees. There were cottages and what looked like an inn. There was a keeper's cottage with children playing beside it, then the house itself: stone, with mullioned windows, and a muddled, grey, forbidding exterior. Huge chimneys. Topiary. A big gravel drive up which they swept smartly.

Surtees had been talking affably and familiarly through the glass partition, which he kept open. But as they arrived he closed both the partition and his mouth, and presented her only with his half profile, of a reddish rock-like appearance which she could see in the driving mirror. They did not stop at the front door, but went on, round to the side of the house where there were offices and stables. Everything looked messier here. Through her half-open window she could hear the sound of carpentry. She wanted this part of the drive to last for ever, and had a strange aversion to ending the journey begun so whimsically at Eastminster.

Admittedly, forgetting her status, she had thought it would end slightly differently. She had visions of walking through a large hall, of greeting servants as though she were a rich foreign emissary, of beginning her stay, at any rate, as a guest with perhaps a long cooling dinner between herself and Miss Oldcastle at a big mahogany table with candles and shadowy shutters.

None of this happened. She was ushered out of the car, up some steps, into one of the offices. Here she sat, amidst a clutter of furniture and untidy cushions, staring dismally at the back to front glass lettering on the door for nearly ten minutes. Surtees had deserted her after depositing her box beside her. She had tipped him, still thinking of herself as a guest. Eventually a woman came in and rather cursorily asked her business.

'I'm the new maid,' said Elizabeth. Try as she might to be playing a game, the words seemed to burn her tongue. She felt ridiculously impoverished, but was certain that the game would rather quickly declare itself to be in jest rather than earnest. It was so ridiculous. She wanted to add, to prevent things getting out of hand, 'actually, I'm a trained psychiatrist' but did not. There was no point in panicking so soon; besides it was only part of her holiday, weird though it was all turning out to be.

'Name of Greycliffe?' The woman's voice, like her face, was hard and expressionless.

'Yes.'

'Elizabeth Alice.'

'Yes.'

'Sign here.'

She signed. It was only a game but she felt as if she were signing her life away.

'Miss Oldcastle won't see you till after dinner. This is a list of your duties. When you've read them I'll show you to your room. My name's Hall. You'll be Greycliffe to me.'

There was a hint of belligerence, no hint of an apology.

'Hope you're better than the last.'

'I hope so too.' There seemed little to say. She read through the list with her heart sinking. This was paid labour. She was in service. Later she was shown to her room. It was small and sparsely furnished, tucked away in one of the house's towers — a little turret room. It could have been enchanting but it felt like a prison.

'Skivvy'll bring you hot water at seven.'

Elizabeth looked around in vain for signs of comfort. There was a cracked washbasin, a bit of a mirror and a tall, hulking dark wardrobe, a narrow bed, chintzy faded curtains, a sampler by the bed:

> God keep you safe throughout the night
> From candle until morning light.
> When you awaken kneel and pray
> God keep you safe throughout the day.

The sampler was decorated with birds and candles in red and green. In another setting it could have looked cheerful and homely, but here it reminded her of Hood's needlewoman:

> With fingers weary and worn
> With eyelids heavy and red,
> A woman sat in unwomanly rags
> Plying her needle and thread.
> 'Stitch, stitch, stitch' — she hummed the lines to herself.

The window was more like a porthole than a window. Shadows flickered across it as if it were under water. She thought they were the shadows of trees, then realised they were birds. They were house-martens, nesting in the gables above. Well, they would soon be gone with the summer. She stood, her shape held in sunlight, rendering her dress transparent around her lovely form, looking out. Far below she could see the cattle. She was tempted to open the window, pushed it and found that although dusty it opened easily, and gazed down on the thick dusky sunlight with rooks and pigeons flocking and calling to each other. Far away there was a glimpse of the sea.

There was a little desk with some lilac notepaper. It seemed foolish to cry but she felt lonely and depressed, and she took a leaf and penned a brief note to Nigel to say she had arrived.

> Castle House
> Near Otham
> Thursday 2nd Sept.

Dearest Nigel,

> I arrived here safely by train. A man called Surtees brought me with my box to the house. It is very strange. I shall need you to write to me, and perhaps one day in the not too distant future you will be able to visit. There is nothing to report at the moment, but I am to meet Miss Oldcastle after her dinner.
>
> With much love,
>
> L.xxxx

She put the letter in an envelope and wondered how she would be able to post it.

Surtees had mentioned tea. But there was no sign of any. She felt tired and thirsty and still a bit awkward on her ankle. After a while, when she had brushed her hair for the third time in the hope that it would make her feel relaxed, a bell rang, turning over a cardboard circle in a box by the door. She went out into the corridor. It stretched lengthily before her. There were some dusty stairs to negotiate, then a green baize door. So far she remembered her way, but on going through the door faltered at the baffling array of other doors before her. It was a long time before she found the one housing the staircase; before she did she discovered that the gallery was full of echoes and whispers — a whispering gallery where even the susurration of dress was picked up and magnified.

Eventually she found the staircase, which was mean, narrow and painted brown. She stumbled down it and found herself in a little parlour. Some tea was set in a cheap pink chipped teapot, with a pile of thin, rather greasy bread and butter. But she set to with an appetite. A pot of home-made jam alleviated the bread which was shop-made and not particularly fresh. At the end of the meal a maid bustled in and took the remnants out through a curtained door. Elizabeth could hear the slapping of crockery. It must be the kitchen out there, she decided.

She looked at her watch, though there was no need, there

being a big oak clock ticking audibly in the parlour. It was six thirty p.m. Miss Oldcastle would not require her presence until after dinner. She decided to go for a short walk in the park, if she could find it.

Finding it entailed a long walk around the gravelled drive past the offices in the fading light, but eventually she found a way out through a barred metal gate. The park was mainly meadow, dense and sweet with clover. There were elderberries and blackberries in the hedgerow. A fat brown snail struggled across her path; she stopped, picked it up by the shell and placed it with its colleagues in a long luscious patch of grass already dew-soaked. The cattle were being called in for the evening milking, and she could hear their distant lowings. Across the meadow, at some distance, was the grey tower of a church and she vowed she would visit it tomorrow. She did not see, just before she turned round, a man shadowing her, nor see him duck into the hedgerow as she made her way back, though she passed a tramp who wheedled some money from her as he sat in a comic caricature of a hat and brown stained, sockless feet among some nettles.

She had returned before seven thirty, and now sat in the parlour waiting for her first meeting with Miss Oldcastle. It struck her that she should have brought some knitting — except what, and for whom, should she knit? Something was necessary to settle her long, pliable, capable hands, which were now trembling with nervousness. She had continually to remind herself of her real status, but at every moment she felt herself thrust back into a past that she had forgotten about, if she had ever imagined it except in books. She wanted to write to Rex, but decided it would be previous of her; besides she had nothing to say except what she wanted to say to him simply. She wondered if in some way she were on trial — on approval; found the thought tantalisingly strange but a bit repellent.

The call came promptly at eight thirty. Elizabeth rose from her seat, adjusted her dress, and was ushered through a hall and some double doors into a large, shadowy stateroom. At first she though she was alone. The room was high-ceilinged and speckled with candlelight. The curtains were partly drawn, and the candles threw reflections into the near-dark outside. There were tall-backed chairs and a long table. It was very much as she had imagined in her first fantasy of meeting Miss Oldcastle on arrival. There was no sound. A log fire was breathing its last in the grate: there was a strong sweetish smell of wood smoke — pear, she imagined, or perhaps cherry. There were no shutters, but tall curtains, partially drawn. All was dark within: dark wood, dark shadows, dark shapes in the further recesses, a dark bottle on the table. For a moment Elizabeth felt like Alice; wondered if she should approach the bottle and if she did so whether it would have a label saying 'DRINK ME', or whether a genie would leap out. She moved uncertainly about the lower end of the table, wondering whether her duties included snuffing the candles out, and whether, if she did so, she would be able to see better in the gloom. She was about to sit down in one of the chairs, then she thought better of it, went back to the door and stood by it — a slim wondering figure, face and hair palely lit, hands clasped before her, waiting for the arrival of the lady of the house.

There was a dry cough. Elizabeth started, then thought it might be the ashes setting and crackling in the dying fire. The cough came again. Peering into the gloom she barely made out a figure, sitting not at a table but bolt upright in a window-seat in the shadow of the curtain. To Elizabeth's surprise she was small — small and dark and doll-like. She had expected somebody bigger and more alarming. She hardly knew what to say, was preparing a speech beginning, 'You called, madam' when the old lady stood up briskly and thumped the floor with a stick.

'Come here. Let me see you.'

Elizabeth moved forward into the light of the fire.

'Humph,' was the next reaction. 'Younger than I thought.'

'It is his aunt,' thought Elizabeth, advising herself to have courage. She moved forward again.

'Come right up to me.'

Elizabeth moved forward again, went past the table up to the figure in the seat. She was grasped by a bony, nervously intent arm which embraced her eagerly.

'Feel my bosom.'

Her hand was guided to the place.

'Does my heart beat?'

'Yes madam.'

'Huh. Hearts. Mine's *broke*, missee! Broke like an old watch. Sit down, sit down.'

There was a scrabbling of hands, and Elizabeth felt herself being dragged down. She sat reluctantly. The hands began to swarm over her, as though reading Braille.

'Young. Well-formed. Nervous. Pliant. Not with child. Is she ticklish? *Is she?*'

There was a frenzied, insect-like tickling movement over her body as though an army of ants were storming her ribcage.

'I'm childless, I am. Childless and sick. They say it makes you sick being childless. Never believe 'em. Doctors! T'other one wasn't childless, not she. That's why she had to go. You're a child too. I can feel it. You'll have to go as well. Up, up!'

Elizabeth rose to her feet.

'Can you dress?'

'Yes, madam.'

'Can you *un*dress?'

'Yes, madam.'

'Can you undress me?'

'Yes, madam.'

'Here? Now! Good heavens ring the bell, what will the girl be doing next? Ring the bell. Ring the bell. RING THE BELL!'

The last instruction was shouted. Elizabeth moved away uncertainly, moved back, found a rope thrust into her hand, pulled it automatically.

After a while another woman appeared in the room.

'This one's no good. She's just threatened to undress me.'

'Yes, madam.'

The woman withdrew.

'There you are you see. None of 'em trustworthy. What brings you here? What do you want? How *much* do you want? I'm very rich you know, ha ha, I don't think. Poor as a church mouse. Death duties, you know. When I died they mortgaged me out in death duties. Very funny. They all want a piece of me.'

There was another cough, tinder dry.

'That cough's me heart. Now let's get down to business. How old are you?'

'Twenty five.'

'Twenty five. Let's see, that's a quarter of a century, oh that's very old. Half way to fifty. Guess how old I am.'

'Impossible to say, madam. In this light . . .'

'Impossible to say, madam. You're a machine, not a girl. Seriously, how old am I? Do I look old?'

She thrust her face at Elizabeth, who stepped back in alarm.

'Tut tut. Nervy type. Go on girl, speak my age.'

'You're younger than you seem,' said Elizabeth. She had caught a twinkle in the black beady eyes.

'Never mind my age. Let's stick to business. What brings you here?'

'You do, madam.'

'I do madam do I madam? Oh madam! Oh crikey madam! The car brings you here, not I, is that right?'

'Yes madam.'

'*Of course* it's right, it always is. Whatever is is right, who said that?'

Elizabeth made no answer.

'The Pope said it of course. The little Queen Anne's man. Now didn't he? Do you think I'm crippled?'

'You carry a stick,' said Elizabeth carefully.

'I do, I do! Very perceptive. I can see we shall strike it off admirably. Only twenty five and says I carry a stick. The world's grown three heads. Get this right in your addled skull, my girl, the stick carries me, is that understood?'

'Yes,' replied Elizabeth, her mind reeling.

'Yes madam, tinderhead. The stick carries me. Now that's settled we can talk business. How much do you want? Seriously, in a large round lump sum. How much of my death is your duty? I'm under arrest, you know. Cardiacally speaking. My heart died when I was, oh, twenty five let's say. Have you a family?'

'A brother, madam.'

'Mother, father, sister, aunts, uncles?'

'None madam.'

'What, all dead? Well you *are* a lucky girl. They pull you to pieces you know. Like pulling wings off flies. Well, well, so you have a brother. Never mind. I'm sure he'll be dead soon. Now let's to business. I need a maid — an experienced maid who knows the ropes: pull the bell.'

Elizabeth delayed.

'*Pull the bell!*'

Elizabeth pulled. The woman appeared again.

'Oh Jenkins, lucky thirteen. This one's fine, she knows the ropes.'

'Good, madam.' Again the woman withdrew.

'You see how it is. Always listening. Waiting for the ticker to stop. Well this ticker's going to tick them into the tomb. The silent tomb. Who said that?'

'I don't know, madam.'

'*You don't know*? You don't know who said the silent tomb? Ah well. Neither do I. Are you a virgin?'

'Yes, madam.'

'Ha ha ha. Yes madam.' A violent fit of coughing. 'Hear that cough? That's the lions in Trafalgar Square roaring. The last one was a virgin too. I'm a virgin you know. Everybody here's a virgin. That woman was, I'll swear it, even though she's got a family. I had a lover once. I like your appearance, number thirteen. *That's* an unladylike thing to say, ain't it? Never admit you like their appearance. Rose's book of etiquette, chapter six. Twenty five and still a virgin, Lor! Good evening, Miss Greycliffe.'

'I beg your pardon, madam?'

'That's it. End of interview. You're the wrong kind of girl for me. This was all a mistake. Lady's maids. Phtt! Scum of the earth. Never trust one.'

Elizabeth stood still, baffled.

'You may go.'

'Go?'

'I know you've only just arrived. You may go. Don't pull the bell. There, there I'm only teasing. I like you. You may stay. Do you have references?'

'Yes madam, I'm fully qualified.'

'Do you have a solicitor?'

'Yes, Mr Welsby of Maidenfield.'

'There, there I shan't need him. Are you a needlewoman? A *clever* needlewoman?

'No, madam, but I can learn.'

'You will have to indeed. Can you read?'

'Yes, madam.'

'Indeed.

 "Still glides the stream, and shall for ever glide;
 The form remains, the function never dies."

Read me that.'

Elizabeth repeated the words.

'Very nice. It's a stream, you know. I like reading about streams. One of the little Queen Anne's man's defects.'

She tapped her forehead. 'No streams. Now you read me something.'

'Here madam, now?'

'Here and now, madam.'

Elizabeth looked for a book. There were none. Her mind went blank for a moment, then she recalled what Rex had said so strangely. She began: ' "In the second century of the Christian era the empire of Rome comprehended the fairest part of the earth and the most civilised portion of mankind." '

Miss Oldcastle looked at her intently.

'Did you make that up?'

'No, madam.'

'It sounds a bit wordy to me. You will have to read me poetry.'

'It feels like poetry to me madam.'

'Not to me it doesn't. Too wordy. Never mind. No novels. Now put me to bed.'

'Immediately, madam?'

'Immediately, madam? Yes immediately. Anywhere. Here if you like.'

'I scarcely know ...'

'You scarcely know anything. T'other one knew too much. Always in extremes. Ah well. Heave ho. Humph. Up the winding stair. Fetch me Fletcher.'

'Your Fletcher?' she said in confusion.

'Fletcher. He carries me when I'm not well. I'm not well, Miss Greycliffe. Ring the bell.'

Elizabeth pulled the rope. Once more the woman appeared.

'Madam.'

'Fletcher.'

'Madam.'

'There, there Greycliffe, you may leave me tonight. I shall make do. But tomorrow mind I shall want you sharp at five. There's a party. Five sharp, remember. Now you may leave. Immediately, girl, don't stand there gawping! Immediately!'

Elizabeth left, gawping, as her employer expressed it, internally nonetheless, imagining the shouting carcase being carried up who knew how many stairs to its unimaginable bedroom. As doctor and as girl she was baffled by the encounter. She had imagined something different: an old lady, perhaps a bit eccentric, but with nobility in her blood, but not this, this *ruffian* — the word exploded from her surcharged consciousness, used as she was to awkward patients. It was partly the fact that she was no longer in a controlled environment, but was, perhaps for the first time, feeling the stress of being alive. She no longer had the collective support of the hospital, the rock-solid assurance that sanity existed among others. The grounds of her being were challenged.

She returned to her room, still simmering. There was little to be done tonight, but tomorrow she could, and did, pen a letter to Miss Oldcastle, informing her stiffly that she felt unsuited to comply with the terms of the service and would like to terminate her employment.

She thought of Rex, then thought he might not have seen his aunt for years. Surely he could not wish that she should suffer — and not merely suffer but suffer these indignities. She thought of him in the boat and the quaint seriousness of his appeal. Surely he had intended something different — or if he had not why did he wish to torture her in this way? The idea that after all it was some kind of game came again to her mind. Once she thought daringly, suppose Miss Oldcastle *were* Rex — and stifled the thought immediately. In some way, she guessed, he wished to expose her to England, as though she were not exposed enough already. Something she had once read about an ideal who was 'a child among pleasures and a woman among pains' came to mind. Well, he was taxing her with difficulties she scarcely knew her way among. Until now her life had been her life — accidental, no doubt, but of value to herself and to a certain extent to other people too. Now it felt like a life in a novel, circumscribed by other wills, other manners, other modes of being. From simply existing as a random molecule with things precious to herself she was being forced into the pattern — not so much of a heroine, though all her natural sense would have resisted that peculiar form of type-casting — but of a paper-cipher, a being compelled into an identity where she might prefer other kinds of freedom. In the hospital, strange as the idea might sound, she functioned as part of a *troupe*, and was happy to do so. Here she was an individual, and already a very lonely one.

The letter was returned with a note on grey paper stuck in to say that resignation was not acceptable to Miss Oldcastle.

IV

It was a day of burning heat, airless, oppressive and blank. For hours she sat shuttered in the coolness of her tower, gazing out on the scene below and around — a scene which was stupid with sunlight. At one o'clock after lunch she had taken her promised walk to the church. It led her past trees heavy with cider apples, through fields of basking hops, past gardens dense with late roses and weighted with globular hydrangeas, where birds sang with exhausted scrappy parched whistles, into a lane. There was an old coaching inn on the corner, called The Boot, with a weatherstained, cracked, fragmented painting of a piled coach. The old road to London must have led through here. Now it was dusty and deserted with low chalk embankments and shallow yellowish flinty soil. At one point she stopped and knelt to smell a ragged white rose that bloomed sweetly in the hedge and nearly bruised her knee on one such stone: angular, horned, projecting like a tooth from the ground.

    The flintstone church was cool, filled with flowers and nearly deserted. One or two old ladies in red hats and grey or brown coats with pins and neckerchiefs sat or knelt in the pews, and one more was active about some business such as collecting hymn books and rearranging flowers. It was too early for the harvest service, but everything was moving towards that devout consummation of the year. The trees in the churchyard were filled with ripening custard apples, the grass was long and thick with seed; beyond the dark green hedge field after field of golden wheat billowed seawards, streaked silver white clouds with the thin breeze that panted from the south-east. Looking back before she entered the church she caught a brief glimpse of the grey gables of Castle House looming under the magnificent pomp and circumstance of high silver white clouds with thoroughfares of brilliant blue teeming between them.

Someone was playing the organ. The soft boom and swell of a Bach voluntary flooded the recesses of the church with music like an inland sea. She thought of Rex, but this organist was silver-haired and clerical. As she left, she noted a wren, adding its piercing sweetness to the soft requiem.

On reaching the house she walked for a while on the soft velvet green lawns, and among the arbours and trellises of the gardens. The gardener at any rate knew his job. Nectarine and peach clung precariously to their battened trees; by the mellow goldy-red brick wall were the soft balls of the apricot. A stream flowed among the gardens, zig-zagging here and there, its music warbling clear and bright as if making the sunlight that sparkled on it audible. There was a cascade with ash-white satyr-like figures carved into a grotto. She stayed there, allowing the cool water to splash her dress and bare arms as it rinsed through the long green translucent weeds that lay in it like mermaids' hair. So cool was it that she was tempted to take off her shoes and stockings, kilt up her skirts and paddle. She did so, watching the silver bubbles stream through her toes as she stumbled about on the pebbles and gravel bed. The pebbles hurt her feet, but the gravel was softer and she could dig her toes in, feeling the soft stuff shift as it betrayed her whereabouts. There were drifts of weeds and once the skinny flick of a fish's tail. Her legs were ivory white, and the water itself seemed to nuzzle them tenderly, with strange fluctuating shifts from clear coldness to drifts of luscious warmth, when the current itself seemed to grow languid and stayed to touch her.

Later she walked among the chicken coops, listening to the cluck and stir of the flecked golden birds with their red combs and fierce bright green eyes. Some of the hens were brooding and murmuring over their nest-boxes; meanwhile the cockerels were strutting and braying over their domain, flourishing great silver-black or greeny plumage.

Throughout this time she was alone, yet never quite lost the sense of being watched. The house had so many windows, some oblong, some circular, some projecting, some recessed in grey free-stone that it would scarcely have been surprising if she were overlooked.

Once she came to a long fence that ran along a field. There were men working in the field, who stood up from their bent postures and gazed at her. She could see a man on a tractor, studying her intently from a distance. She wondered how many people knew of her arrival, and assumed that Surtees must have sown gossip broadcast. It never occurred to her to think of him as Mr Surtees, which was odd, for Elizabeth was unfailingly polite, even in her mind.

Later she returned to her room, and sat awhile in a sort of trance, half-thinking, half feeling, waiting for the summons at five. The sun lay thick as paint on the prospect, and sounds penetrated with preternatural clarity through the dense, dust-laden air. Once she heard the click of a metal gate; at another time it was the sound of sawing so close that it buzzed in her ears like an enormous fly. Some lines of Tennyson came to mind:

'... but most she loathed the hour
When the thick-moted sunbeam lay
Athwart the chambers, and the day
Was sloping towards his western bower.'

Then she did not say, 'I am very dreary', but she felt the weight of a whole purposeless afternoon lay on her like a physical body with all the willed solitude of a monastic idyll. She longed for the stir of voices, the fun of her brother, the idealism of Rex. She took up notepaper and began to write to him, but the words would not come.

At four thirty she went downstairs to a washroom which she shared with the other servants and washed in cold water in a sink fed by a big tarnished brass tap. She changed her dress and applied splashes of perfume which made her smell soft and flowery. Then she waited.

Had she been in a noticing state of mind she would have seen that as evening came on all the clouds had stagnated and were building in the west, and that the seaward clouds had teased and tuffeted themselves into high mares' tails until the sky looked like an estuary or delta with high bright patches and darkening flats with pale sky between.

Punctually at five the bell rang and she made her way along a corridor and through the gallery to Miss Oldcastle's dressing room: a grotesquely disproportionate room with heavy oak appurtenances.

The lady of the house stood at her dressing table by a

mullioned window, flushed with the flare of the setting sun. There was at first no conversation, and Elizabeth, embarrassed by the scene of the previous day, carefully removed Miss Oldcastle's day dress, stockings and shoes, feeling as she did so how slight was the form that submitted to her attentions — how thin and birdlike the arms, and how lightly the heart beat in its bony cage.

'There, there,' said Miss Oldcastle pettishly, 'I can wash myself, you know,' and she proceeded to lather herself in cold water.

Then, in a brown dressing gown, she drooped into her chair before the mirror, muttering to herself: 'Puffs, patches, bibles, *billet-doux.*'

'Pass me my Bible, Greycliffe.'

There was a storm of papers on the dressing table. Elizabeth hunted through old newspapers, clippings, bills, letters, and books; at last found the Bible and passed it to Miss Oldcastle, who riffled through it contemptuously as though to say 'Don't tell *me* these things.' Elizabeth knew instinctively what was demanded of her. She stood behind the chair and began arraying Miss Oldcastle's hair. It was very thin, and required to be tied behind.

'I'm a ruined Jehovah,' remarked Miss Oldcastle conversationally; 'don't pull so hard. This is now bone of my bone, and flesh of my flesh.' She was looking at one skeletal hand.

'Not much flesh, eh, Greycliffe? Not like your hands, eh? Very fleshy they are. Funny how God enacts his history from the beginning on every new generation. You'll see: once the bone starts biting the flesh. For dust thou art, and unto dust shalt thou return. Which reminds me. Polish that table. Before you do so pass me those sermons.'

There was a black book on the table. Elizabeth passed it to Miss Oldcastle who put it in her lap.

'Polish away.'

'There's nothing to polish with, madam.'

'Use your hands girl, those plump lazy pigeons. No, ring the bell!'

Elizabeth rang. After a while a girl's head appeared enquiringly at the door.

'Beeswax and besom.'

The head disappeared.

'Don't stop. I like to feel your fingers in my old excrescences. Ha ha, only twenty five! When you are as young as I am, Greycliffe, you shall say, "Would God it were even!" And at even you shall say "Would God it were morning." What does a rolling stone do?'

'Gathers no moss, madam.'

'Correct! But what does that mean, eh? Gathers no moss?'

'Picks nothing up.'

'Very true. (Don't *tug*. I dread to think what Lady Coley will say.) Is that all it means?'

'Madam?'

'Madam indeed. You think about it, girl. Gathers no moss. Faster. If ye had not ploughed with my heifer, ye had not found out my riddle. Hear this, Greycliffe, hear ye I say. "Temptations take hold of us sometimes after our tears, after our repentance, but seldom or never in the act of our repentance, and in the very shedding of our tears" — Idle nonsense, I never shed tears. Do you shed tears, Greycliffe?'

'No, madam.'

'I should think not indeed. O, drop the briny tear with me, ha ha, scarcely. Daisy, Daisy give me your answer do, I'm half crazy, all for the love of you. Scarcely very intellectual. Unlike tears.'

The girl returned with a tin of Cardinal polish and a yellow duster. Elizabeth took them and placed them on the dressing table.

'Very tasteful. There amidst my things. Your chore for tonight, girl. Before midnight this room must be sweet and wholesome with wax. Now the pride of the wicked is to conceal their sorrows — why? That God might receive no glory by the discovery of them. Extraordinary thought. That old buffer lifting the lid on secret sorrows! I said in my haste all men are liars. Do you know my nephew?'

'Madam,' said Elizabeth miserably, trying to pile the thin hair.

'Mr Rex Buckley, he sent you didn't he?'

'Yes, he did, I'm afraid ...'

'He he! *You're* afraid. *I'm* afraid. He sent you, I'm afraid. Do you know him?'

'A little, madam.'

'Don't pull so viciously. A little madam knows my nephew. *Bats!*'

This was said ferociously, with a jab at her forehead.

'I beg your pardon.'

'I beg your pardon. Woe is me that I sojourn in Mesech. He sent you. Do you know why?'

'No, madam.'

'He's bats, that's why. Don't trust him. Do you know what he wants?'

'No, madam.'

'He wants my money and your body.'

Elizabeth drew back.

'Ha, that stung you didn't it? Little miss do-me-no-harm. A whip for the horse, a bridle for the ass, and a rod for the fool's back. Miss Greycliffe, you're a fool, and your fingers are hard on my back. Let's see, let's see. Hopeless. What kind of fashion is that?'

'It's my fashion,' answered Elizabeth proudly. 'It is how I like best to see my own hair.'

'Her own hair, in faith. Curly locks, curly locks, wilt thou be mine? Thou shalt not wash dishes nor yet feed the swine — is that how he wooed thee? — Oh, beware of men's silver tongues, my dear Greycliffe, because later it's I'm the king of the castle, get down you dirty rascal. He sent you here to wash dishes, you know. To get those fat, soft, pliant, plump, goluptious fingers bony and worn in preparation for being a woman. Home is the woman's workhouse, did he tell you that? I bet he didn't. Oh damnable, deceitful man. Now my tiara.'

Every fibre in Elizabeth's body resisted but she pressed the head piece into position.

'Hopeless.'

'Why, madam?'

'Feels rotten. All lumpy. Try again. No, still hopeless. Ah well, grin and bear it. You've ruined my evening, Greycliffe, I shan't forget this. Sir Kenneth Dumberwell, the Chief Constable, Lord Lacie and Captain Robinson of the *Queen Elizabeth*, accustomed to the ravishments of my appearance, what will they say? Miss Oldcastle, how ill you look! All on account of my new maid, gentlemen, gentlemen. How old do you think I am?'

'Indeed madam, you look . . .'

'Silence! I address the company. Lord Lacie? "Indeed madam, you look older than the rocks, ninety three if you are a day." *Ninety three*, my lord? Why I'm a girl! It's all on account of my new maid, gentlemen. Give me my gloves. *Stipendium peccati mors est*: and what is so intricate, so entangling as death? Only my new maid, gentlemen. How intricately she entangleth me, she and her lover bold. I'm a bobbin, gentlemen, spun with strange elastic threads. There, that's enough, you've done your worst. Ring the bell, and polish, polish, polish till the dead of night brings lead to your golden cheeks. Ugh, you're beautiful, I can't stand you near me. Havers, this woman offends me, take me down, take me down out of her sight.'

Only the sense of being caught up in a play — either a play of others' inventing or the play of mind that comes to people suffering terminal illnesses of the brain, had kept Elizabeth civil during these last moment. Despite the conversation, despite the rudeness, despite the violent and wracking references to her lover — as she suddenly and momentously thought of him — she had kept her mind focused on the art of dressing, and had made, as she thought, as attractive a job as possible out of difficult material. To have her efforts dashed aside as worthless brought tears to her eyes as surely as if a hand had struck her. She imagined the feelings of a colt being heavily bridled for the first time and beaten by a groom. Another girl in her situation had asked, 'If this is the beginning, what will the end be!' — a sentiment Elizabeth unknowingly shared.

She waited and polished and waited. It was impossible to know whether Miss Oldcastle really had company, or was hoodwinking her further with a show when in fact she was dining alone. Though the thought of Miss Oldcastle dining in state alone was no consolation. By midnight when the door jerked open, the room was as clean as it had ever been, the papers sorted and stacked, the furniture gleaming, the dressing table sweet with polish applied and shone with vigour. All sense of real time had disappeared. She felt she was living a dream where time had become a shadowy outrider of someone else's company, galloping where she would amble, and dawdling interminably where she would gallop.

'Number thirteen, still at its exercise. Why girl, the house is asleep!'

Miss Oldcastle sat, without further comment, in her original chair. Her hair was still piled high, the tiara was on, jewels bedecked her arms and the bosom of her white dress. She looked abominably impressive, like an Aztec temple.

'Take it off,' she said, 'take it all off. It doesn't please me. It is only to please the gentlemen. Ah! gentlemen.'

Her face was streaked with weariness. Elizabeth felt some stirrings of compassion as she went to her. They were instantly stifled.

'My nephew was there, of course.'

This was news indeed.

'Really, madam?'

'No, not really. I *felt* him to be there. I felt his beady eyes on my locket all night. Take the locket off. Look at it.'

Elizabeth removed the locket, carefully unfastening the clasp. It was heart-shaped in tarnished silver.

'Open it if you will.'

'I would prefer not to, madam.'

'Open it.'

There was a picture inside: a tiny colour photograph, faded, of green and flesh colour.

'Do you recognise him?'

'Recognise who, madam?'

'The face.'

'No. Yes.'

'You should. Pease porridge hot, pease porridge cold, pease porridge in the pot, nine days old. It isn't him, you know.'

'Him.'

'Yes, him. Well it isn't. You thought it was, didn't you? It's his father. That's my brother so it was. A bad 'un. A pain in my little finger. Prick, prick, prick. His son's just like him. I feel him hereabouts.'

She pressed her side.

'Thorn in the flesh. Give me the locket. No lock it away. There. In the little chest. With the silver key. My jewel box. I'm fearfully rich. He won't get a penny. I told Lacie. He wasn't there either. None of them were. None of them will. Benwell's on my side. My solicitor. He knows the ropes. You had a solicitor, what was his name?'

'Welsby, madam.'

'Tut, a speck. Benwell will crush him. Are you aware, Mr Welsby, that your client is an adventurer? A fortune seeker?

A tuft-hunter? There, that's enough. Undress me. Oh lord your fingers are soft. Touch me there. And again. Oh lord, that's better.'

Elizabeth undressed her as carefully as she could. The jewels were all put away, the dress removed, the nightgown prepared.

'I want a flannel. And cold cream. Always cold cream at night. It keeps the complexion so fine, don't you think? A maid's face must come out of a jar. Do you take liquor? There in that drawer. That's the one.'

The drawer was opened and a bottle of a golden appearance with a black slanting label was discovered.

'Glasses, In the same drawer. That knotty one, that's mine. You take any of the others. Nothing idle about being rich. Always busy. Do you play the stockmarket?'

'No, madam.'

'And you don't drink. Oh, goody two-shoes, too good for this world, aren't we? Do we smoke? No we don't. Well *we* do. Hand me a cigarette. From the next drawer. Light it for me.'

The cigarettes were in a green and gold packet. Elizabeth selected one. It had a gold band round it.

'There that's better. Now I shall smoke myself to death and you shall go to bed. Immediately, Greycliffe, Greycliffe.'

'Madam.'

'You aren't half bad. Madam this, madam that. Oh, little madam. I love teasing you.'

'Shall I go now?' asked Elizabeth.

'Of course. Fill my glass. Directly. Have you seen me say my prayers?'

'No madam.'

'Of course not, girl, I never do. Prayers. Who should *I* pray for? Myself, no doubt. Good night Greycliffe.'

'Good night, Miss Oldcastle.'

She retired, leaving the grotesque figure in a state of undress, sucking on the white and gold tube, and swigging whisky. Retired in a state of exhaustion to her turret, where she undressed and fell asleep immediately.

Some time during the night she awoke. The peculiar promise of the weather had not been unfulfilled. Rain pocked and pimpled the pane of glass, accompanied by a strange gusty sigh from the trees — a weird rushing sound that sucked and fluttered the curtains outwards, grew until it howled in the chimney and rattled the door, then wavered away into silence, like a tide flooding and spilling in the orifices of all the house's many caves.

It sighed and soughed or hissed sometimes like a sharply intaken breath, or gurgled and rattled like an old man with laryngitis. A tree began an insistent tattoo on the wall directly below the window, making her think fearfully of Miss Oldcastle's stick coming down the corridor towards her. All the spectres of the house, all its myriad skeletons, were awake and coming out of their closets. She shivered under the bedclothes as though someone were walking on her grave.

After a particularly violent gust there was a click. She could just see through the gloom that the door stood ajar. It would have been the work of a moment to close it but she lay still transfixed by the thoughts that *someone was in the room with her*. There was a gust of cold air that shivered her whole body, and there were fingers at her throat. She wanted to cry out but the nightmare pressed down on her body, rendering it unworkable. With a violent spasm she heaved herself up, to find Miss Oldcastle standing in the room with an axe.

A scream throttled in her throat — a huge silent scream in which the horrors of the day fought for expression. A myriad thoughts flashed through her mind, fractured and fell to pieces, as if a looking glass had shattered in her brain.

The shape did not move, but it spoke.

'I hate you. I hate you so bad ...'

Now it did move. It lifted the axe with surprising speed and brought it crashing down on the foot of the bed.

'Don't,' said Elizabeth in suffocating tones of entreaty. The figure laughed. 'I get possessed at times, number thirteen. Is this your lucky day?'

Again she raised the axe. This time it descended but very slowly. Elizabeth had time to think of the strange power that could control such a heavy weapon before it embedded itself softly in the bedlinen beside her.

There was another laugh. 'A trick, an old trick. Don't you think I'm clever?'

Elizabeth's brain flashed a message to itself. 'She's asleep. Do not disturb her.' She said nothing but awaited the third blow.

It did not come.

Instead the strange form was in bed with her, licking her face and kissing her.

'Oh my dear. Oh Miss Greycliffe darling, I'm so ill.'
She smelt of whisky but did not seem to be drunk.
'I've brought a piece of candle. There, in its stick.'
The figure wriggled violently and there was a rattle of matches. After several attempts the candle burned with a sick, smoky, fitful flame. Miss Oldcastle took the candlestick in her hand and flared it towards Elizabeth's face.

'Now let's examine you. What a lovely face. Why is it lovely when mine is old? My skin is in tatters, hers is like silk. Look at the sheen. Beauty is hard to identify.'

The fingers prodded Elizabeth's face.

'Real flesh. See the blood come and go in it. Her pure and eloquent blood. Issuing with tidings from her heart. Where's her heart? All nestled away no doubt. Sleeping with a young man somewhere, I'll be bound. Oh! Here it is. All softly embosmed. Such a sheen on her everywhere. Yet that's not it.'

The axe was shifted uncertainly, then left to lie.

'Let us anatomise beauty bit by bit. Let us pull beauty to shreds with our fingers. Why should some possess it and not others? Does God damn a woman for an ugly mug? Mine's ugly enough. I would I could find the secret of hers. Is it the warmth, I wonder? Some bodies are warm through and through. She breathes everywhere. Every pore is a part of parted lips.'

Frenzied kisses were lavished on Elizabeth's neck and bosom. She lay very still.

'Yet that's not it too. Is it the proportions?'

A hand folded over one half of her face.

'I could quarter her face yet not find the secret. Is her nose beautiful? Pooh, it's a piece of flesh with bone in it like mine. Is it the expression? Yes, it's in the expression. Her eyes are startling blue and clear. They look you through, whereas I can only squinny. That means she means no harm. How strange it must be to mean no harm. To know you're good. Now that I flatly deny. What about the cripples? Are they all damned? A corrupt notion. Just for having no cast in her eye. I could make mincement of her for having no cast.'

There was a pause. The bedclothes were tugged away.

'Her legs are very elegant. Now there's a peculiar notion. We're descended from the monkeys and find elegance in a limb. Wherein does that elegance consist? In smoothness. How hairless her legs are. She must shave them. That sheen everywhere. I wonder what she eats. The calves are very finely proportioned. Agile and neat. Look at her ankles! A pure-bred filly. These are called thighs. Now that's a most peculiar word. Old English, I wouldn't mind betting. The upper part of the leg: why should that be beautiful? It must be those delicate blue veins — oh, very delicate: I could kiss one if it were considered seemly: which of course it is not. Except in the Song of Solomon of course. Let me kiss thee with the kisses of my mouth, for thy love is better than wine. Thy belly is like a heap of wheat set about lilies: fair even there. No, it's none of these, it's in that expression. Funny how she sleeps with her eyes open. That blue affrighted look. Some ghost of tragedy lurks about the brows. Very fair and clear, her brows are. Indescribable that look of beauty. Some ache of being. Look how dark and liquid her eyes are! I could drink at them. Agape. Startled. Haunted. How can an expression be both open and haunted? Well, her's is. I'm only scratching the surface. How can beauty elude me so? I want to possess it, to ransack its secrets.'

There was more frantic kissing.

'How she withdraws. I shall say my prayers. At her side. Perhaps she will make me good. Let's see. I haven't said a prayer for years. How do you begin? Dear God — no, that's no good: too informal. I doubt if the Deity would be very pleased with that. He's very busy, you know. The Catholics have a good idea. They pray for the intercession of the saints. I suppose this will be a rather profane prayer. Here at the shrine of beauty I dedicate myself, etcetera etcetera. God bless mummy and daddy wherever they are — come! That's a good thought, I felt an instinct of grace. She doesn't know how graceful she is. That's part of the secret of her beauty. She gives me music in the head. Dah, dah, dah, dee, dee, dee. Very classical. Very highbrow. Makes my head ache. I wish my brow were as high as that. Why is hers so high and mine so low? A prognathous accident? A quiver with the forceps at the crucial moment of delivery? Come, it's none of this, that girl's a princess and no maid, yet she is a maid. A queer conundrum. Where does she come from? What's her parentage? What's the secret of breeding? Nature above its station? I should ask my nephew. He's the clever one. He'd say it was the genes. Baloney. Genes have nothing to do with it. It's in the quality of potential. Potential for grief I'd say, that's the clue. She looks as if she could grieve. Well, I've prodded and petted her enough. She might wake. Then were'd we be? Shall I leave my friend in bed with her? *Carte de visite*? Scarcely. She might find it. Then we'd have a rare to do. Boohoo, I want to go home. Darling, this is your home now. I'm your friend, dear number thirteen. Your very own friend that I've been waiting all these years to find. Well, you may love my nephew if you can find him. I never know where he's at. Of course he's engaged. What! You didn't know that? I could have told you straight away. Well that *has* dashed your ducky dream! Look at your face now. All fallen, but still so beautiful. Men smirch their womenfolk at the moment of contact, didn't you know? Well, it's better you should know from me. I'll preserve you. I'll work on you until you think in my way. It's better so. We maids should stick together. Look at you, all blithe and debonair. You don't know how to persecute 'em. I'll bet he said a little word and she said yes. Foolish dreamer. Foolish, foolish dreamer. I'll teach her to scout those dreams, yes I will. She shall never dream again while she is here. The candle's guttering. Time for bed. I would stay here, I would, and quaff my fill of that strange stuff beauty, drain it to the dregs. How the storm raves! She dressed me well tonight, no-one will ever know. To bed, to bed, says sleepy head. Come on old friend, old joe metal-head. Suppose they found you here. They'd put me away yes they would my friend. Nobody knows of you except me. They'd put you away too. Burn you on the fire. Come on old joe, back to our lonely chamber over the gate. Back to bed, joe-axe, back to bed!'

The weight on the bed lifted. The candle was blown out. The door closed with a stealthy click.

Elizabeth lay stunned. Only her idea that the woman was asleep had prevented her from screaming. She lay bathed in perspiration, baffled as to what to do. Some things that had been said left her heart all jangled like chimes pulled awry. There were some notes of pity mixed with it all. Whether the old lady had really intended to murder she could scarcely tell. She knew she would be well out of it as soon as possible, yet to go and leaver her in this state . . . Was Rex really engaged? Why had he not told her? It was cruel of him to deceive her, as cruel as to ensnare her in this terrible game. Even if he trusted her. In her nightgown she slipped out of bed and switched on the light. It dazed her eyes. The sweat was drying on her, leaving her cold, shivering and clammy. The thought of that — of that *violation* of her body! Even with a man she scarcely imagined it could be worse.

She was at her desk. The words tumbled over in her mind. It was her first loveletter and it was desperate. 'Dear Rex, help me to escape,' was what she wanted to say. Would he reply? Would it even reach him? The house was like a sealed unit. They must scrutinise the mail. She thought of him on the beach, so arduously helpful. Dearest Rex. Dear Mr Buckley. Everything was wrong. He should not have asked her. She hadn't thought it would be like this.

Dawn came up and discovered her still at her desk, the letter unwritten but the paper all scrawled over as if with a mad woman's writing. The storm had blown itself out and everywhere in the parks and gardens were new lakes of light-filled water.

V

The news of a new arrival, particularly in an area as closed as a village, provokes gossip; more so if the arrival is a girl; more so if she is pretty. News of Elizabeth spread in uncertain ripples outward from the mouth of Surtees and other members of the house down to The Boot. There they splashed unevenly into inquiries about 'the neat liddle girl up Miss Oldcastle's way' and finally made their way in wavelets to the front dooor of Hudson's farm.

   Mr Hudson was a big cheerful old fashioned farmer who specialised in dairy products. His gold and white Jersey cattle roamed the fields and marshes almost as far as the sea, supplemented by soft woolly Southdown sheep. His big whitewood and brick house sprawled sleepily around the edge of Otham as if it owned the little town. Big and cheerful he was, yet with something grim and unyielding in his disposition, as if the work of farming — the continual supervision of his herds, his flocks, his men, the big wire fences that ran round the perimeters of his fields, the continuous inroad on his finances by feeds, and tractor fuel, and rates, and dips and expenditures of all kinds necessary to preserve the great sunny farmlands that visitors saw left him not exactly drained of inner resources,but defensively wary of them. He was the farmer in the tractor whom Elizabeth had seen during her walk, and who had stopped in his duties to observe her picking her way prettily around the confines of the park. He had been married once, but now his wife was dead. Two sons were in London, doing well in stocks and shares; one of them was Miss Oldcastle's financial adviser — a thankless job since she was so capricious and ungraceful in her decisions. He had a daughter too, younger than either of the sons, a girl named Adeline who was bright-faced and nervously flirtatious. She kept house for her father, knew the neighbours, was intimate with all the gossip and was partly the subject of it. 'It is a truth universally acknowledged . . .' When Mr Rex Buckley had appeared in the neighbourhood several years ago it was universally acknowledged by Adeline Hudson and her gossips that whether or not he was in possession of a large fortune — and certainly Miss Oldcastle's ways left you in doubt as to whether she would die a millionaire or a pauper — he must certainly be in want of a wife. He had the starved look of a bachelor. Adeline felt herself peculiarly equipped to deal with bachelors. Not only were her brothers, as she saw them, temporarily free-fliers in a world essentially governed by women, her father too, despite his status as a widower was also, as she saw it, fundamentally a member of that distinguished sect. His loud cheerful laugh and the seams on his forehead that buckled like braces under the pressure of good and bad news alike were no defence: underneath Adeline saw a solitary man in need of good feminine keeping and she did her best to keep him in that state. She banked him down like a good fire, making sure that the hearth of the fire was always burning for her own especial warmth.

So when the new arrival came there was double danger spelled out for Adeline. Danger to her father and danger to Mr Buckley. It was Adeline's task to draw the teeth of this serpent, by ensuring that her influence extended no further than the house — yet if it remained *in* the house goodness knew what harm might be done. Suppose this Greycliffe became an heiress! A preposterous thought, yet Miss Oldcastle was a crank, they all agreed. It was not a truth universally acknowledged that an old lady in possession of a good fortune would necessarily settle it on the most deserving aspirant.

Adeline thought long and hard and decided that an invitation to tea was in order. The girl must be lonely up at the big house day after day with no company. It would be preferable if her father were not there, for occasionally he rebelled against her intricate disciplines and called her a minx. So the tea would be earlier than usual. But not too early in case the girl possessed a clear head. There were times when it was good to have a father to rely on, even if he was a bachelor by temperament.

Adeline penned the note in her best handwriting. She waited for a reply and received one — rather gracious it seemed, as she thought somewhat sniffily, on lilac paper. Oh my goodness, lilac paper, my dear, she told her best friend, another farmer's daughter, not quite as prosperous as herself, called Miss Cartwright. Cartwright was a slightly downmarket name, redolent of cartwheels and donkey work and it suited her. However, for the time she decided to suffer the absurdity of lilac notepaper.

Miss Greycliffe had said yes.

Preparations were awkward. An element of display was involved, yet would it seem appropriate for a mere lady's maid? Appropriate or not it was decided on. The food was to be mainly provided by the cook and would consist of scones and cakes with fresh jam and cream to which Adeline was particularly partial. The bread, however, would be cooked by herself. Flour and yeast were bought from the granary shop that morning. Everybody in the village knew her; this was very comforting. 'Shopping again, Miss Adeline?' 'Yes, just a little experiment in cookery. Some bread this time.'

'Your father always praises your bread.'

'Oh, my father . . .' A pretty laugh was in order.

'Doesn't know when he's well off, do he dear.'

'Scarcely.'

She swept out of the shop in her straw hat and pink dress with an air of triumph.

Breadmaking was an accomplishment, and Adeline was accomplished to the finger tips with which she sometimes condescended to touch the piano. With her sleeves rolled up, she plunged her arms in dough, sifting and kneading it energetically. She knew she looked very well at such moments; besides, she loved the big warm spacious kitchen, with its glittering copper implements, the big checker-clothed table, the black-leaded range, and the smell of cookery and garden things all mixed up together. The storm a few nights ago had torn some roses down and the cook had been quick to transplant them in water to the kitchen, where they bloomed and scented the air wonderfully.

The cook was busy baking in her red and blue dress with a big white apron, and Adeline, prettily dressed in pink and with an apron to match, was emulating her. When Elizabeth arrived there was an entrancing smell of — as Adeline put it — new mown bread. It was immediately apparent that the new arrival was somewhat pale and shy and in need of being bucked up. Adeline chivvied her to inspect the oven, and even to help her take the bread out. It lay warm, crusty and cocooned in cloth on the kitchen table, sweating slightly from its ordeal.

They were to eat at four; in the meantime there was the farm to be inspected. The inspection entailed much traipsing over wheel ruts and visits to pens where grown calves were lowing and bulling each other. To Elizabeth, after her enforced seclusion at the house, it was a visit into a pastoral wonderland. She followed every bird, every winged thing with her eyes. Once a butterfly settled on her arm, and once, to Adeline's great amusement, a ladybird lighted on her chin and crawled downily into her hair, tickling her face. 'It looks like a beauty patch' she said. She removed the bug delicately with her fingers.

'Oh don't crush it,' said Elizabeth, 'give it to me.'

She placed it on the back of her hand and whispered a rhyme over it. The ladybird took wing, shining momentarily golden in the sun, then zigzagged drunkenly away towards a pile of steaming compost.

By four o'clock the girls were great friends. Adeline led Elizabeth into the house's inner sanctuary, a big cool room with lace on the comfortable armchairs, where she presided over the teapot. It was Adeline's deepest wish to hear of life up at the house, but her new friend was singularly uninformative. She pressed for information about Miss Oldcastle over buttered bread and scones but Elizabeth had little to tell her. The ideas that were paramount in Adeline's head were wills and solicitors and Elizabeth's head was full of the problems of farming.

After a while Adeline switched her attack. It seemed unlikely that Elizabeth was immediately a danger as far as money was concerned: what about suitors? She rang several rather delicate changes on the nature of young men until just after five when her father came in. She was very glad to see him. He stumped into the hall and changed his boots, then made for the television room, but she headed him off and forced him to come in and shake hands. He did so awkwardly, as though he had changed hands after farming and the new pair did not fit properly. He gazed down at Elizabeth from a great height. She was intensely aware of his presence. Big and bony, rather dark, with deep-set eyes — she was sure it was the farmer who had gazed at her so intently from the tractor. She flushed, feeling he had somehow contrived to see her wading in the stream. She answered his questions politely, remaining, however, muffled on the theme of Miss Oldcastle and her vagaries.

'Tis said she's a termagent. Many young ladies haven't stayed the course.'

'I'm not sure how long I shall last,' laughed Elizabeth, 'but at the moment she is my employer.'

'Where'd you come from?'

Elizabeth told him. He looked perplexed.

'You don't speak like t'other girls.'

'No,' said Elizabeth cautiously.'

'A bit too up in the world like, if I may say so.'

'Not very up, I'm afraid.'

'Hard taskmistress, is she?'

'It's a slightly peculiar position. A friend sent me to look after her.'

'Ah. She needs looking after sure enough. Don't you think so?'

'I think she does.'

'Needs a bailiff bad for her grounds.'

'Hasn't she got one? The gardens look very nice.'

'Ah. Grounds go to waste.'

'That's a pity. Though I did wonder if and how she managed such a huge estate. By herself I mean.'

'We all wonder that, Miss ...'

'Greycliffe,' said Elizabeth.'

'Miss Greycliffe. We all wonder that. Times are hard on landowners everywhere.'

'Even on you, Mr Hudson.'

'Even on me, miss.'

'Oh Father,' said Adeline.'

'Tis true Adeline, you don't see the sweat every day that goes to keep you in fine linen. A girl never notices these things, Miss Greycliffe. They think land's for keeping ponies on.' He stroked his daughter's head unconsciously.

'There. Don't pet me, Father. I know as much as you about farming.'

'He laughed. 'I would you did, girl. Farms are where bread's made, isn't that right?'

'Yes. And wheat is grown. And cattle live.'

He laughed again. 'Now you've seen it all, Miss Greycliffe. Farming takes place within these four walls. If you don't mind my asking, which friend sent you? Do you know what the old lady most needs?'

'Those are two difficult questions, Mr Hudson.'

'Answer them in turn. Take your time.'

'The first is easier to answer in any way. Her nephew sent me.'

'Mr Buckley?'

'Yes.'

'I know Mr Buckley, we all know him down here. A fine gentleman.'

'Yes.'

'But a bit of a dreamer, wouldn't you say?'

'Yes. I don't know. He seemed . . . '

'Oh, Rex Buckley *seems* all right,' said Adeline. 'But look at his family. Seeming is nothing. He seems to have a good enough head but when you think what's in the blood you wonder.'

'Well,' said Elizabeth, 'we all have things in the blood . . . '

'Yes, but I *know* Rex Buckley!'

'Do you,' said Elizabeth warmly. 'He was very kind to me once'.

'Oh he's kind. He's kind to everybody. A proper — what's the name of that book with donkeys?'

'Donkeys?'

'Yes, you know.'

'Travels with a donkey,' said Elizabeth helpfully.'

'No. Donkey something. It's a man. He tilts.'

'Don Quixote?

'That's it! He's a proper Don Quixote, always tilting at things. Don't let him tilt at you, Miss Greycliffe — oh you're blushing. He has, hasn't he?'

'Adeline,' warned her father. 'take no notice, Miss Greycliffe, 'tis an interfering creature.' But he too was fascinated by the rich subcutaneous colour of the girl.

'No, he never tilted,' said Elizabeth. 'But yes, it was his idea.'

'And a strange one!'

'Yes, I suppose in a way strange.'

'There you see, Father, I knew he was involved somehow!'

'Girls,' said her father. 'If you could spend on the farmyard the amount of mental 'rithmetic that goes into counting wild geese we'd be a sight richer. A darned sight richer.'

'Mr Buckley is my friend, Miss Greycliffe. One of my special friends.'

'Very special?' asked Elizabeth.'
'Oh very special. We were almost engaged ....'
'Adeline.'
'Well it was true, Father.'
'You never told me.'
'There are some things a girl can't tell her father. We were, Miss Greycliffe — very nearly. Until I broke it off.'
Elizabeth's head was spinning but she pressed on.
'The two questions are related.'
'For me there was only one question, but two answers. I said yes, then I said no. Do you think that was silly?
'I scarcely think ...'
'It is very hard for a girl to decide. It is, Father. You men scarcely realize the hazards. I was thinking about children. Then I thought about that *thing*.'
'That thing.'
'Up at the house.'
'Yes but ...'
'Adeline, you go too far too easily. Pour me some more tea and let's hear no more of your silly nonsense. Why if I'd ever dreamed that Rex Buckley was courting of you I'd have ...'
'What would you have done, Father dear?'
'I'd have banned him from the house. There, 'tis said. And with my apologies to Miss Greycliffe.'
'No apologies are needed, Mr Hudson.'
'Girls say too many things too easy. Not you, I'm sure.'
'Would you really have banned him from the house? How exciting. I wish I'd been there. What would you have said, I wonder?'
'Well I wonder too. I've nothing against the lad personally.'
'None of us has. He's a very nice man. But that old thing ...'
'Needs looking after,' said Elizabeth. 'She's a very sick woman. As to what she needs, I'm not sure. Care and attention of some kind, I'm sure.'
'Care and attention! She needs a thump on the head. She's had enough care and attention to last a lifetime. My impression is she's a thoroughly selfish old lady who hates us all. Sometimes I feel that the whole county is on the side of Miss Oldcastle and I wonder why.'
''Tis because she's old and a lady. Now pour the tea and let's hear no more of your carking.'

Adeline did so and tea was finished in a querulous silence on Adeline's part and an absorbed silence on the part of her father. He scarcely knew what to make of this new arrival. She seemed very graceful and, well, beautiful, he had to say. After tea he slipped out of the house and returned about six with a bundle of flowers — dahlias, chrysanthemums, ox-eyes and Michaelmas daisies. He thrust them at Elizabeth, a trifle churlishly.

'For me,' she said, 'Oh how lovely! I shall put them in water as soon as I get — back to the house.'

'Home, you would have said.'

'Would I?' she said gaily.

'You seemed to falter over it.'

'Yes. As soon as I get back.'

'Miss Greycliffe.'

'Yes.'

'Take no notice of us and our ingrown ways. We gossip and gossip but no harm gets done. Gossip takes care of its own weird ways so long as no scandal comes of it. We like to protect one another and do so well enough in a crisis. This here is a good home. Share it if you like. Day may come when you're glad of a roof over your head. This is a good roof.'

She looked him full in the face. He looked away awkwardly.

'They say you do a good job up there.'

'I scarcely know how. Scarcely survive. If you see Mr Buckley tell him I should be very glad to see him too.'

'*I* see him!' He laughed rather bitterly. 'If you know him yoursen, you'll be the one to see him. I scarcely know the lad. I should like to know what he's up to, submitting such as you to his mad pranks. I'd get him to provide for the old woman with a proper bailiff. That's what she needs the most of, choose how.'

VI

Elizabeth became a frequent visitor at the farm. Sometimes she took tea with Adeline, who had taken it into her head that it was her job to teach Elizabeth to ride. She provided her with jodhpurs and a pony named Melody. Despite the name Melody proved to have a cantankerous temper and a tendency to bite sideways at great mouthfuls of air while cantering, like an eccentrically angry crawl swimmer. After some days of practice they rode as far as the coast and watched the sea, which was grey and muddy with rollers, returning tired and sore late in the afternoon.

At other times she went for long walks with Mr Hudson, listening gravely to his prognostications about winter wurzels or his weather lore. Once he took her to a coppice where he was chopping up firewood. He asked her to place her foot on a bough which he was sawing. She did so, feeling a pleasant tingling go through her body as he strained in shirt and braces with a big bow saw. Everything was lethargic with heat. A wasp half drunk with cider juice bumbled into her hair, and as they walked back she had endlessly to brush away the clouds of gnats that rose around her face.

Her mornings and evenings continued to be employed in the usual routine at the house, submitting to Miss Oldcastle's vagaries of temper, her whims about dressing, her dinner parties fantastically garlanded with names. There was still no word from Rex or any sign as to how soon her strange ordeal would terminate. Sometimes she wondered if he intended her to give up her job at the hospital altogether and wrote several letters explaining how awkward this would be before dismissing the idea as impossible. Yet the long silence made her fear that he had some such notion in mind. To be there for ever! The other people were, of course, but she didn't belong to them, however hard Mr Hudson tried to make her feel at home.

At home! Had she known Mr Hudson's mind she would have felt less at home than ever. For Mr Hudson was in love with her — infatuated with her. It was her simplicity and gravity that attracted him. He scarcely knew where to turn, either for her or without her. Strange that a middle-aged farmer should be discovered carving a girl's initials in the bark of a tree, yet Mr Hudson was to be seen doing this one hot evenning after a visit from Elizabeth. He ached with desire for her, and the fact that he had no articulate ways of expressing his desire only made it worse. Unconsciously the girl had ignited a long slow-burning fuse in the man.

Is sexual infatuation worse for a woman or for a man? It is a strange condition, where the world goes dark and immobile except for the brightness of the desired object, who remains an object rather than a person. Mr Hudson could scarcely bear the idea that Elizabeth had other lives, other modes of being, to which he was a stranger. He was jealous of his daughter, jealous of the pony, jealous of the clothes she wore. Once, when the girls were riding, he had gone to the room they called her room, and found her skirt, soft blue and silky in texture, laid neatly out on the bed. He had buried his face in it, smelling the soft evanescent perfume of her body through it. Another time, Elizabeth had been allowed to stay for the night; the next day she was gone, but again he found a pretext to go to her room and touch and nuzzle the slight moulding in the bed and pillow left by her form. He groaned under the weight of his desire; his dark eyes bolted in his head, looking wild and animal-like with frustrated longing. He revered her.

He became morose and savage, cold-shouldering her in a clumsy hope that this would somehow make her pity him. He took to long solitary expeditions in the woods when she arrived, sometimes returning unexpectedly with a brace of bloodied rabbits, which he threw down on the table in a kind of fury. Yet the flowers continued to arrive. Elizabeth's room at the house was always fragrant with them.

Is sexual frustration worse for a man or a woman? A woman can feel it, yet in some ways is prepared for it. She has a closer relation with sexual things than a man. Her clothes are chosen for that very purpose. They fit and flatter her figure. She has confidants, she is expected to act flirtatiously, her tongue moves more easily in her mouth. Mr Hudson had no such outlets. He was not a vain man, had no interest in his appearance; his clothes lay on him as if on a naked savage. His fundamental interests were commercial; even his sense of the seasons was governed by a sense of financial reckonings. He had no outlets for passion except shooting, getting rich, and indulging in increasingly fantastical imaginings about her clothes. On cooler days, when she wore a soft grey woollen coat, he wanted to be the coat and fasten himself in gold at her creamy throat. Her belts obsessed him, hugging her form as they did; he imagined himself a soft belt in black leather with big silver buckles which would hold her forever — or until she threw him off in favour of some looser garment which he would likewise become. Faintly he imagined the sensation of being her petticoat and feeling the shape of her body and thighs as she walked beating against him. Sometimes he was the wind, moulding her as sunlight moulds fruit, until he groaned with the beauty of her, and ground his nails into the palm of his hand until it bled.

No physical action was too arduous for him, yet no physical action but left him feeling drained, weak and unsatisfied. In company he desired solitude; in solitude company. He yearned to do beautiful actions in her sight — to translate sun and air, to be a hero, to perform great tasks: yet being a man of limited or stunted imagination and of sturdy self-mocking commonsense he found no outlet there. The commonsense which had carried him through life as a successful business man, strong and unemotional in sensible transactions, now became a terrible stumbling block to deeds and imaginings of worth.

He thought at one point that he would open all the sluices on the marshes and drown the grazings until the waters rose as high as the house. Then, on horseback he would carry Miss Greycliffe away — but where? In shooting animals he shot at the something in himself that was obdurately prosaic and asked for reasons. His obdurate self laughed his romantic self out of countenance. In the evening, before bed and the torture of night after night without sleep, he would encounter a face that looked hale and lumpily expressionless, like a swede. No sight of his suffering appeared except in the eyes that burned blackly like sullen coals.

His daughter became afraid of him; his fits of sullen temper grew worse. His attitude to the men changed. Before, he had worked as one of them, seeing no obvious dividing line between the farmer and his hands. He assisted them in all their work. Now everything changed. He became aloof, moody, unsatisfied and angry. Nobody dared joke with him any more — he would turn on the joker with a snarl and say 'That's a dam-fool statement, Tom Crick.' They learned to suffer him in patience. He turned his back on his neighbours.

He read very little except for the Bible and Bunyan. Once he came across a phrase in the latter — *I could have blessed the condition of the dog and the toad* — and underlined it in heavy, faltering pencil. It was his condition exactly.

One day his daughter came to him with pent-up excitement.
'I've discovered her birthday: it's tomorrow!'.
'Her?'
'Miss Greycliffe's.'
'Ah.'
'Tomorrow, Father. Shall we give her a party?'
'You may, my dear. So long as I shan't have to take part.'
'Father, what's the matter with you? You're so cold and hostile to everybody. Is it something I've done?'
'Ah. Happen not.'

Nevertheless he slipped away and bought a gold cross at a jeweller in a nearby town. Then he brooded over it. It looked very snug in its white cotton wool and its cream box. He snapped it open several times, imagining the touch of the cold fine chain at her neck, and shivering slightly as he imagined his thick fingers at the clasp. If he stood behind her he would gaze down the front of her dress. If he stood before her he would gaze into her eyes.

'For me?'
'For you.'
'Oh, how lovely.' That was what she always said when she received the flowers.

Then he kissed her. Her eyes went misty with passion, her red lips gaped for his. Then he laughed shortly and snapped the box shut.

Strange her lips were. As if they were crying. Her mouth was wounded somehow. Quivering.

He did not give her the cross. The next day he buried it in one of his drawers among his shirts. But all day until she came he kept finding pretexts for coming into the house and fingering it.

They had a special tea and she agreed to play the piano for them. It was Adeline's piano, a nice small upright in white wood. Mr Hudson knew very little about music, his acquaintance with the art being mainly limited to hymns and the roaring choruses of harvest home songs:

> It came upon the midnight clear
> That glorious song of old
> From angels bending near the earth
> To touch their harps of gold.

That or:

> So jolly boys now, here's God speed the plough
> Long life and good health to the farmer.

She sat down and touched harmonies that were strange to him. He watched mesmerised as her hands negotiated the keyboard. They were like swans, white and graceful, but surprisingly decisive.

'What is that, Miss Greycliffe?' he asked docilely.

'It's Beethoven. The *Pathétique Sonata*.'

'Beethoven.' He outlined the name with care. 'I thought he was German.'

'He was. But the music has a French title. It means it's full of pathos.'

So many strange names and words. A German composer who wrote in French. She must be cultured to know so much.

'Beethoven.' he said again, imitating her pronunciation. Then there was that other word. 'What's a sonata?' He pronounced it 'senator.'

'Sonata,' she said again. 'It's a piece of music in several movements, like a very concentrated dance suite.'

Dance sweet! This music didn't make him want to dance. It made him want to weep, though they were tears more of frustration than of pity.

She played again, this time the *Moonlight Sonata*. She explained why it was called 'Moonlight'. He couldn't understand how moonlight should be in music. Nothing so silent as the moon.

'Half moon t'night,' he observed at a point of silence. 'Soon be harvest moon.'

'Father!' shushed Adeline.

Secretly he longed for a jig. But he loved seeing her sculpt music out of the keyboard.

When she finished he clapped. 'Very nice. But more like a thunderstorm than moonlight, I'd say.'

'It's only the first movement that's moonlight. It's not a very good title. Not very apt'.

She used words very finely.

'Now Adeline must play.'

'Oh no, you continue.'

'No, Addie, it's your turn. You play us a reel or a jig and show off your pretty voice.'

Adeline played some country songs. She sang *Barbara Allen*. The lovely tune got mixed up in his head with thoughts of Beethoven.

'Them great composers didn't know so much about tunes,' he wanted to say, then thought of the wrapt stillness with which she approached the music with French names.

She played again, this time some Bach. It made him sit up a bit.

Jollier, that fellow than t'other one.

Then he relapsed into moodiness. Again he left the room and went upstairs. They heard him stumping about over their heads.

'Your father's upset about something.'

'Oh don't worry, he's often like this.'

He was fingering the cross, muttering 'Bach, Beethoven, senators, queer kind o' dance, 'cept she sets my heart dancing, not in any way I know of.'

Then he went out and picked some flowers.

'For me? Oh, how lovely. You spoil me.'

That was it. He did want to spoil her. Part of him wanted to sully her, almost to manure her into his land.

'Just a birthday offering.'

'Mr Hudson.' She held him lightly by the hand. He could feel her fingertips cool as tulips in his harsh red paw.

'We're friends, aren't we?'

'Ay, always friends.'

'Yet you aren't as you were.'

'Aren't I?'

'Are you unhappy?'

It was a daft question. Either she could see he was or she couldn't. In that case she should leave him alone.

'It's the time o' year. Always anxieties about this time, specially when weather's changeable. Too much rain rots a good harvest. Then there's combine to hire. Baler. Men to pay. The year's never settled for the farmer. Always time to pay, never time to play.'

Elizabeth sighed. She was unable to penetrate the reasons for his moody temper, but felt unhappiness everywhere. It was in the air. It must be autumn. The year taking farewell of itself.

Once again she walked back to the house. Although only September, the leaves were turning yellow and falling, and making themselves loam in the earth that was never unrained on long enough to be unmuddy. The green of the house lawn was again before her, blazing with flowers at its edge, and looking from a distance like a vast fallen leaf, bitten into by vivid browns, yellows and reds. It festooned the ground before her weary eyes. Everything was amiss. Even the smells got mixed up in her nostrils, making her sneeze as though she had contracted hayfever. Playing always left her troubled in blood as though the music had entered her body.

Brushing her hair that night she found a thread of silver. It made her sigh as though the hair were not hers at all. The idea of things whitening down into winter and the unimpassioned sleep of impotence.

It was time to face the hardest problem — what to do about her stay at the house. It was time to write to Rex.

She faced the letter with the greatest reluctance. To write to him at all was a task, to write to him with any kind of business in mind, when he was essentially all she had in mind was to compound a task into a kind of farce. To have to relate her feelings to complicated questions about other intentions meant that the letter was doomed to be an absurd failure. She could not bear that the one important letter of her life should be so hedged about with conditions that would virtually turn it into a matter of question and answer. Nevertheless it had to be written. There was bound to be an element of reproach about it, for she had expected more assistance from him — had expected things to be made clear for her, not confused.

That evening she set to, spreading out the notepaper before her, dreading even the task of calling him by name. To know so much and so little!

Castle House,
Near Otham,
Friday 8 September 1963

Dear Rex,

I scarcely know if you remember me. I believe you do and that you were sincere in what you said; as was I. I felt those things too, Rex, and though frightened by them am prepared to stand by them.

Dear, where are you? I need you very much. I am very baffled here. I do not quite know what I am supposed to be doing or what you would have me do.

Rex, you must know I cannot stay here for ever. My holiday will soon be over, and then what? I cannot easily walk out on your aunt for she seems to depend on me.

It would be possible for me to say that I have got involved with a very intractable case who needs my constant care and attention — I think I could gain more time in that way. Also that there are rather delicate personal reasons for my not returning immediately. If only I could say there was a sickness in the family! Believe me I nearly feel it as personally as that.

Does this seem overfamiliar? Sometimes I feel you are at my elbow, sometimes that you are a thousand miles away.

Dearest, there are some problems of management at the house. It is thought by Mr Hudson, the farmer, that Miss Oldcastle needs a good bailiff to manage her land.

One other thing has come to my attention. I do not know how to mention this. The daughter of Mr Hudson the farmer, who is very nice I think, said that she was once almost engaged to you. Is this true? If it is are you sure you are no longer contracted to her in any way? It is not only that I should hate to stand between you, but that I should hate anything of that kind to be between us.

Miss Oldcastle is I believe very ill intermittently; sometimes she seems all right. I am in a very strange position with her: she treats me exactly as a lady's maid would be treated. It is like going back in time a hundred years or more. At least I now understand how the Victorian governesses and servants must have felt!

Rex, was it this you intended? Did you wish to punish me

in some way for being insensible to problems that are alive? I can imagine you feel that by putting people in hospital we somehow cauterise their relationships with life. The sick should look after the sick — is this what you mean? Or that we are creating a society that likes to forget about sickness by consigning people to asylums?

Yes, I am learning all sorts of things, not least about myself. If I had been a Victorian I should have been looking for my Mr Rochester.

Is that why you will not come to me? That I must learn another gamut — learn a different music?

Please write to me soon, for I need your advice and need to feel you by me.

With much love
Elizabeth (Greycliffe)

It was not very satisfactory, but it was a letter of sorts, and made some attempt to bridge the gulf that she felt. It could not, however, express her loneliness. She sent it in a letter to her brother, also asking for assistance, and for a word from or about Rex.

Then followed the nightly ordeal with Miss Oldcastle who did not know it was her birthday, and would not have cared if she did.

VII

Langley's
204 Borough Road,
Eastminster.
Sunday 10 Sept.

Dear Liz,

I got your letter. It all sounds very strange. I thought Rex was with you. Well, I told you he's a queer chap. He went away, you know. Left me in my lameness. (Here followed a picture of a man with a stick.) I must say I should like to visit you. WOT LARX as the man says in Dickens. Do you think the old lady's mad? It sounds fun from a distance. I've got a rotten cold. All this sea air does you no good. My leg's a lot better. How's yours? Better completely I bet. Have you been swimming? I miss watching Miss Porpoise. All these misses and bets. Seriously, isn't Rex there? I did think he'd be around. I don't altogether know him, though I'd trust him anywhere. I wonder if anything's wrong with him. How long does your holiday last? It sounds like a busman's holiday. I've got serious plans too — for an office block. How serious can a man be about office blocks? I expect they'll want the usual thing — tiled like a public lavatory and with a modern sculpture outside to prove it's all in the cause of art. I thought of a design in yellow brick. Very bold and flash. My coffee's getting cold. I'm not really writing this at Langley's but at the coffee bar up the road — you know, where we sat that afternoon.

Keep well, and don't let them work you too hard.

Love
Nigel

She laughed. It solved nothing, yet it was like a breath of fresh air. If only there had been some news of Rex. What could have happened to him?.

She sat in the library, which was full of dark bound volumes. It was her job to prepare some poetry to be read to Miss Oldcastle. She thought she would read Tennyson. It seemed the right time of year.

> The air is damp and hush'd, and close,
> As a sick man's room when he taketh repose
> An hour before death
> My very heart faints and my whole soul grieves
> At the moist rich smell of the rotting leaves —

that, or *The Lady of Shalott:*

> In the stormy east-wind straining,
> The pale yellow woods were waning,
> The broad stream in his banks complaining,
> Heavily the low sky raining
> Over tower'd Camelot.

She looked out. It was very apt. Rain streamed on the Victorian stained glass windows like tears. The trees were threshing and plying, and the air itself looked yellow and exhausted. She thought of Mr Hudson's harvest. It would be rain-ruined. She turned the pages.

> I loved the brimming wave that swam
> Thro' quiet meadows round the mill.
> O the dreary, dreary moorland! O the barren barren shore!

And best of all:

> The woods decay, the woods decay and fall
> The vapours weep their burthen to the ground.

Strictly speaking it was too early in the year. This was the poetry of late October or early November. Yet the glass had fallen and with it had come an oppression in the air.

The library was thick and musty with damp books. Damp everywhere. She stirred restlessly in her dark plum-coloured buttoned chair. Some of the volumes were stacked high out of reach behind wire doors. She wondered what was in them. There were magazines on the table — a copy of *Farmer's Weekly*, a *Gazette*, a *Punch*.

She stood up, leaving the book on the table, and went to the window, unconsciously smoothing her hair.

> A man that looks on glass
> On it may stay his eye
> Or if he pleaseth through it pass
> And then the heavens espy.

The glass was thick and knotty with bubbles and veins. The stained glass, in scarlet, blue and green told little stories. There was St Christopher. There was Ruth, gleaning. Autumn everywhere!

The colour of the glass reminded her of goblets. She would have liked to pick a piece out and to have drunk the rain.

How the rain streamed. It too formed liquid knots and veins and hung in globes on the bushes and flowers. Occasionally a wan shaft of sunlight shone through and made everything sparkle — then a filthy cloud bedraggled itself over the white space in the sky where light came from and everything was brown and dun.

How quiet Tennyson was. That moody voice speaking to itself like nature: fitful, harmonious, ever-darkening.

She struggled with the window latch; tugged at it. It resisted, then suddenly yielded. All was noise.

There was close at hand a steady drip-drip from the nearest shrubs, which were all streaked dark with wet. Further away a restless pitter on the plants and flowers. The wide-leaved plants made a stronger sound like rain on umbrellas. She imagined the gaudy scene like a bank holiday crowd at the races, the bend and sway of light as their feet moved under umbrellas, could see the tic-tac plants waving their arms. The bigger shrubs were horses moving uncertainly in the paddock. Those toadstools under the laburnam were like children —

Baby finger, waxen touches.

A myriad visitations at the door of her mind that vanished

as soon as she allowed them into her consciousness.

Further off the rain rushed on the gravel, and hissed on the meadow.

The sky dragged at the earth, scooping up moisture and, when fully burdened, dumping it elsewhere. The wind moaned among the trees.

Waning, waning, everything waned in Tennyson.

It was her mood. Other things waxed. She mustn't submit to moods in which everything waned. She walked back to the table and made a note on some paper, to the end that she must tell Miss Oldcastle that things waxed in autumn as well as waned.

Her skin, as she stood again by the window, in profile, looking out, was waxen and clear. Strange how white it stayed in spite of the sun. Strange how red the men's skins were in spite of the rain.

Red skins and white skins.

How it rained. It was as though a pipe had burst somewhere. There was a suction of rain, as though elephants were drinking their fill.

Indian summer.

'Autumn moulds the hard fruit mellow' — someone had written that. Tennyson again perhaps.

There were so many volumes, all disused, mildewed, rotting down quietly inside their big leather jackets. Volumes with black Victorian print like tombstones, even though some of them were meant to be festive. Those volumes of *Punch* with long intricate jokes and parenthesis. There were some volumes of a Victorian magazine. Her eyes strayed through it. 'Conducted by Charles Dickens': like a bus conductor. All those buried words. Other volumes. Here was a confident voice:

'ABERGLAUBE is the poetry of life.'

Elizabeth laughed. What was ABERGLAUBE? It sounded like Jabberwocky.

And here was a voice she knew:

'In the second century of the Christian era the empire of Rome comprehended the fairest part of the earth and the most civilized portion of mankind.'

Had he read it here, in this very room? She looked round as though memorising it. The table, with dry spilt stains of ink upon it. The big windowy shelves. The two table lamps of brass with dusty flexes. The three armchairs, in one of which she was sitting. One of them with a patch of brighter cloth. The parquet floor that clattered under her heels. That faded brocade. The persian carpet in faded blue. The high ceiling with mouldings and alcoves.

Strange to think he might have breathed those words from this very volume. Some time ago — it was thick with dust. She moved her hands uncertainly through the thick pages, that fell open for her like Vergilian lots:

'He signalized his youth by deeds of valour and displayed a matchless dextrity, as well as strength, in every martial exercise and even in the less honourable contests of the Olympian games.'

She smiled to herself, thinking of the inaccessible minds of men.

And then:
>All day within the dreamy house,
>The doors upon their hinges creak'd;
>The blue fly sung in the pane; the mouse
>Behind the moundering wainscot shriek'd.

Engaged to someone else. That would be it. A momentary flush of passionate stirring before all the clumsy apparatus of circumstances hemmed him in. He might even now be sitting staring dully at a blank sheet beginning, 'Dear Miss Greycliffe, I should have told you at the time ... '

It made her feel unutterably sad — to think that she might have become, however inadvertently, part of a trap. 'The young man needs his freedom,' something said in her head.

How it rained.

The window was still open. She could feel cold air on her shielded face. That strange smell of rain, as though the ground were opened by it and all its odours were yielded up. Sweetness, then patches of mould. It was as though you could smell earthworms. The smell of darkness.

Somewhere round by the offices they must be taking down scaffolding. She had been listening to the clang of metal and beat of hammers for a long time before she noticed it. It reminded her of how little she knew of the business of the house. There was a crash and a cry.

What did Miss Oldcastle say? The rich were always busy.

Birds were creeping through the undergrowth, looking plumy

and soaked. A mistle thrush was keening from a top branch.

It was strange how every person, every thing was a private space. Yet somehow they were all linked in the intricate pattern people called life. Her being was, she supposed, as unguessable to the people of the house as theirs was to her. She tried to imagine them all going about their duties.

She wondered if they watched her in her comings and goings. She felt very new, scarcely belonging at all, yet already she was accepted as part of the routine. At meals, which she ate in the servants' quarters, they talked to her a bit. Surtees 'joshed' her as he put it. He seemed to find her amusing. He looked at her over his ruddy eyebrows, over his big platefuls of beef and Yorkshire pudding, potatoes and peas and laughed in a way that was open and comradely, yet also somehow closed and furtive. She couldn't tell whether she was supposed to laugh back. Sometimes she did and that made him laugh the more.

'Ay, yer a one, Greycliffe,' he said, bursting his tubes with private amusement. 'We all know yer. You are certainly one.'

He laughed so much that his big pouchy eyes squeezed out tears.

After dinner he lit a big black pipe stuffed with ragged tobacco and told stories. One story made him laugh so much in the telling that she had never heard it. It concerned a big white blue-eyed gander called George. Even Mrs Hall laughed at George the gander.

'No story like George, an' all,' she said, adjusting her hair from the back of her neck. 'Mind, though, how he ended up roast that Christmas dinner.'

'Ay,' said Surtees wiping his eyes, 'he did en fine to the end, did George. Niver fergit is blue eyes when they come for en. Hissed once too often foris own elth.'

There was an explosion of laughter.

Surtees helped himself to pudding, mounding it over with custard, and with a look of modest pride replacing the laughter lines round his eyes.

'Old George,' he said, choking and spitting on the pudding. 'Them blue eyes. What, me next, e says, stretching out is neck. You ain't going for to make a meal o' liddle old me? Oh yes we was. 'E was delicious to taste. Right down to the feet. No they don't make ganders like George no more, Greycliffe. He'd er known you all right. Ha ha ha! Ha ha ha!'

He took a swig of beer, spluttering.
'No beer neither, Greycliffe?'
'No thank you.'
Everybody found that funny.
'Why ain't she the lady of the 'ouse' remarked Ron Tallwood the butler admiringly. He had a deep bass voice and black curly eyebrows. 'Quite the madam. "Naw thenk yaw".'
This phrase caused endless amusement and for a while they all went around in fainting fits.
'More pudden, Ronnie?'
'Aw, naw thenk yaw!
Sometimes Surtees asked her to go shopping with him.
'You don't 'ave to go . It ent the maid's bisnes to go with en.'
But she went. He drove her proudly to the town in the front seat. While he loaded up with groceries he allowed her to walk down to the sea.
'Pick yer up at twelvish like by the pier,' he said.
She walked down amongst the shingle and the groins to watch the waves beating and the gulls flying against the wind. Fishermen were on the beach selling their wares; there was a salt aroma of fish and sea water.
When Surtees came to pick her up he brought some dabs and sole.
'We're very pertickler to these,' he said. 'Nothin' like 'em for unfreezin' the obderate art of All. Eluded my advances for years she as, but she can't resist them dabs.'
He had been drinking; she smelt the alcohol on his breath.
'Ladies is a funny breed. Never understand the 'motions of a woman.'
Once he tried to kiss her. When she struggled free he only laughed.
'Knew you wouldn't, Greycliffe. Too canny for none o' that nonsense, I dare say.'
The tide was low. They stayed a while by the struts of the pier, inspecting the barnacles and marine life. Thick clots of dark weed clung in bushels to the metal framework. As they walked back they passed a jellied eels stand.
'Like some, Greycliffe? Aw, naw thenk yaw! Well, I will. Very partial to that there shelly-fish breed.'
He ordered some cockles and covered them liberally with vinegar from a bottle on the counter. He seemed utterly

unabashed by her. As they walked back to the van he pressed some cockles on her, selecting them specially like sweets for a prize pupil. She tasted them delicately, letting the salt flavour her mouth and the watery vinegar taste seep through on to her tongue.

'Nice eh? Like little leddies. Each with its ticklish parts.'

He rummaged for a handful and stuffed them into his mouth.

'Clamourin' they are to be eaten,' he said obscurely through a muffle of moustache.

She laughed and he laughed back.

'Got any menfolk, Greycliffe?'

'No,' she said, 'at least ...' and let the sentence die.

'At least,' he said, worrying at its tail like a terrier. 'At least 'ow many? Comely girl like you shouldn't be lonesome. Don't like to see a leddy lonesome. Fair makes my art bleed.'

He laughed again.

'Don't take any notice er my ways,' he added. 'Bit low, I 'spect, for what you've come to take for granted. Funny thing, people's opes and expectations. Very ard to satisfy, either in the bulk or in the partickler. Ever bin to a fair?'

'No,' she began to say, 'not since ...'

'Never bin to a fair!' He stared. 'We'll 'ave an outing. One day when th' old leddy's got no tea-parties or nothink. We'll go on the dipper together like. Do you think that'll suit you Greycliffe?'

'Yes,' she said she would like that very much.

'End o' season,' he said. 'See the lights an' all.'

It was arranged. They were all to go. There was a race meeting on a Saturday afternoon. This afternoon. Until the rain came and washed and washed at the terrace. Now she doubted whether there was a chance of their going, and she sat in the library and read, and brooded, and felt no part of the life of anything.

VIII

The park was full of umbrellas and Wellington boots: a mirage of blues and golds, flashes of pink, pale transparencies. Once you were out in it the rain was bracing as it beat against the face. A wild wind was gusting the trees, bending the poplars at their elegant topknots and bullying the oaks. Racehorses looking miserably soaked were being led around the paddock with their coats on.

She was with the people from the house — it still stuck in her throat to call them servants.

There was no racing. The flat land was a sea of puddles and churned grass. This didn't seem to stop people from talking, laughing, betting even; though Elizabeth wasn't sure where the bets were going. Surtees came back once with his face triumphant.

'Nice liddle win at Chepstow,' he exulted. 'Nice n' sunny down there.'

He was sheltering under a huge green golfing umbrella.

'Lay you hundred to one you niver thought we'd make it this afternoon.'

'Two hundred,' she said.

He laughed. 'Fancy a 'amburger, Greycliffe — aw naw thenk yaw. Come with us, we'll find some.'

He strode plashily around the race-course. She almost had to run to keep up with him. There was a fair with noisy bright-coloured dodgems flashing blue and white electricity. The smell of singeing metal swept into her nostrils.

'Others are in the hen closure. Taking cover. All says it always rains on her day off. You like walking, it seems.'

'Yes, very much,' she answered.

'Thought yer did. I follered you when you arrived. All around the house you was. Thought you was looking fer somebody.'

'No, not really, just getting my bearings.'

'See them things?'

'Yes.'

'Know what they are.'

'No. They look terrifying.'

'Fancy a go?'

'I'd rather find a coconut shy.'

'If you shy a coconut I'll take you on one o' them. Waltzers they're called. Proper crool, especially to a leddy. Need to pin your skirts down on them, Greycliffe. Look at 'em fly!'

He stuffed his hands in his trouser pockets and stood a while gazing and laughing.

'Old leddy no trouble today?'

'No. That is she expects me back not too late.'

'Fer why?'

'I have to read her some poetry.'

He exploded with laughter. 'Poetry!' He mimed like a geisha girl:

> My art is like a singing bird
> Oos nest is in a watered shoot.
> My art is like an apple tree
> Oos boughs are bent with fruit.

Thickest fruit, least to say. Didden know I could recite like that, I'll lay. Ow much shall I lay yer? Two 'undred.'

'It's too late,' she murmured, 'I know now.'

'Because the birthday of me life
Is come, me love is come ter me — learned that at school. Never fergit what you learn at school.'

'Where did you go to school?'

'Nowhere in pertickler. You read the old leddy that. Know any Rabbie Burns, Greycliffe — aw, naw thenk yaw! Ha ha ha!

> Auld nature swears, the lovely dears
> Er noblest work she classes, Oh!
> Er prentice an' she tried on man,
> An' then she made the lasses, Oh.

Ain't very biblical-like, Burns, but truer to nature some'ow.

Allus think man's the botched one o' the species. Nature done er work wi' a finer pen when she come to er own. Even All makes a man look cumbersome. Lovely to look at, leddies. Like th' old ships in sail. 'Igh rigged and 'andsome.

> Should auld acquaintance be fergot, Greycliffe,
> An' niver brought to min', Greycliffe,
> We'll take a cup o' kindness yet, Greycliffe,
> Fer auld lang syne, Greycliffe — leastways we'll take

one o' these 'ere 'amburgers. These is poetry, Greycliffe, you tell the old leddy that an' maybe she'll leave you in peace. Tell 'er a 'amburger, lying sizzling and cocooned in a wad of soft bread, lovingly spread with Coleman's French mustard fer preference, ate on a cold and rainy afternoon wi' a comely lass fer company beats all the poetry in existence.'

He gnashed his teeth demonstratively. 'Ave a bite? — Oh, look over there! Darts board. Now if they've got a darts board they'll 'ave a coconut shy. C'mon Greycliffe, lets see yer chanst yer arm.'

There was a rain-saturated canvas tent flapping greyly in the wet, with a few strong men throwing darts at a playing card. Nearby was the sharp noise of a shooting gallery. The air in the tent was stiflingly warm, like a laundry. They wandered through, until they came to the coconut shy. Four or five bearded coconuts sat in their frames.

'Sixpennorth fer the leddy,' said Surtees. 'Now Greycliffe let's see you knock its napper off.'

She took the balls from the man and retreated several yards. It seemed important to do this right. She threw with a rather stately round-armed action as she had learned when playing cricket with her brother. The first balls went wide and Surtees laughed.

'Lay yer two hundred, Greycliffe.'

She held the ball determinedly, feeling its round hard shape in the palm of her hand, then released it. There was a clunk and a coconut toppled out of its frame. Surtees cheered.

They took the coconut and went out of the tent into the rain again. She wanted to take the nut back intact but Surtees pressed her to open it on the spot.

'If I take it back with me we can all share a piece,' she said.

'Oh, *share*, he said contemptuously. 'Give us the nut.'

He took it to a wall-end and smashed it against the corner of a brick, returned with it dripping.

'Ave a taste.'

She drank the white milk thirstily. Surtees watched in amusement.

'Never sin a leddy drink before,' he said. 'Usually they sip.' He took a piece of the fractured white meat and chewed on it noisily.

'Very nice, expecially comin' fro' you. Now fer them waltzers.'

She protested, but he laughed at her. 'It's either them or that beer tent. Now you wouldn't want me to be at the beer this hour o' th' arternoon, surely?'

He led her away. They threaded the loud noise of the fair, watching children with candy floss, and hearing the beat of the steam organs on the roundabouts. There was a black machine with whirling arms and screams coming out of it.

'Octopus,' said Surtees. 'Very exciting. How about the big dipper?'

'No thank you,' she said very definitely, but allowed him to coax her on to the waltzer.

At first it wasn't too bad. They sat side by side in a metal box, with a safety handle that they pulled up towards them and hung on to. The roundabout began to move, slowly at first, and the box stayed still on its wheels. Then the music got louder and the roundabout began to move faster. A man came and took their fares, lingering behind their car. He gave it an experimental whirl. It lurched easily on its wheels. Before she knew where they were they were facing back to front. The car was going up and down as well as sideways. She wanted to get out but Surtees laid a warning hand on her arm. The man whirled them again, faster. The car seemed to shudder sideways as though going down a steep slope. Elizabeth called out and heard the man laugh. He was behind them somewhere, balancing easily on the moving surface. He whirled them again. She felt sick and dizzy, felt her head go down between her arms. Her skirt was flying and Surtees was laughing. She grabbed his arm and clung on. Experimentally he eased an arm behind her back. She drew away in alarm, then the car lurched again and flung her at him. He kissed her easily.

'Mr Surtees,' she protested. He laughed again.

Then she seemed to lose all sense of direction.

The motion eased, the roundabout was slowing. The dip and sway were less pronounced and they were coming to a halt. She tried to stand up, but the motion was still sufficient to throw her back in her seat. Her head went against Surtees's shoulder. He kissed her again. She was indignant, shouting for the man to stop. The roundabout was slowing and slowing. She began to see the blurred faces of the crowd. Were they laughing at her too? She felt too disorganized to care. Surtees removed his arm and squeezed her fingers. Disconsolately she allowed him to. He was still laughing when the chair stopped.

'Easy when you know how,' he said.

She felt angry and hurt. It was a trick. Surtees handed her out. She found she was still clinging to him, dizzy and lost.

'Oh, Mr Surtees.'

'There, there my chicken.'

It was then that she saw Mr Hudson. He seemed to be glaring at her from the crowd. She put Surtees's arm away, wanting to run from him towards the friendly figure of the farmer. But he was gone, lost in a sea of faces. Once she thought she saw his head and ran through the crowd. People stopped and stared. When she came up to him she found it was another man.

Surtees was nowhere to be seen. That was a relief. But now she was alone, wandering here and there in the fairground, still dizzy, hearing voices boom around her, loudspeakers crackle and crash, music volley. Her head was going round and round. She thought she was going to be sick. She was still clutching the remains of the coconut. Why was Mr Hudson glaring so? At the ruin of his harvest?

She wanted desperately to be away from the crowds. Everywhere was quaggy with mud. Water soaked into her thick walking shoes and squeezed down the collar of her raincoat. She put her hands in the pockets; there was water there too. As well as feeling sick she felt deeply offended in some way she could not express. Surtees *should not* have touched her. Suppose Mr Hudson had seen! Emotionally she was on her beam-ends, like a yacht that has put to sea in rough weather. It was borne in gradually on her that she was sailing among the Passions, and that they were inscrutable, incomprehensible and very violent forces, that had no care for her except as an object, and would throw her away like a tennis ball once the furry bloom of her novelty had worn off. She had only her own sensations to hang on to, and they were such fickle and changeable things like the weather itself. It would seem like paradise now to be sitting in Miss Oldcastle's stuffy old sitting room, watching the autumn outside and reading Tennyson.

She had no idea how entrancingly pretty she looked: pale but with the blood flushed in her cheeks, eyes alive and alert, hair escaping in rivulets from her rain hat — a sight fit to turn less volatile heads than those of Surtees and Mr Hudson. Many a head did turn in the crowd as she made her way alone, searching for something, she didn't know what; or somewhere, she didn't know where, beating against the winds of merriment, with a sedate, collected melancholy in her eyes and clutching the wreckage of a coconut. The rain streamed like tears down her face. She looked like a child who had lost her mother, her eyes big with all the collected woes of the weeks.

Small woes, but trivial things make humans of goddesses. She did not know the strength of her beauty, or how being displaced made her finite nature an infinity of possibilities. That was how people saw her — as a possibility amidst their own impossibilities. That was why they courted her, amidst their own difficulties where *Labor omnia vicit, Improbus et duris urgens in rebus egestas*. Perhaps every unplaced person is a god or goddess. Even Surtees had his weird divinity, though it was a divinity of pickle jars and dimpled pint pots. A figure out of pastoral, but with a dauntingly physical presence. Elizabeth's beauty was not physical, it was elusive. Sometimes she seemed ordinary in the extreme, then at other times translucent with the spirit of place upon her. Even here in the mud and commonplace of a country fair she shone strangely like a moon.

Had she known this she would have laughed. For she felt a most impotent moon. Wishing only to draw up Rex in her arms, she seemed to drain the earth in a sieve, pulling tidal passions hither and thither, with the one thing she most desired fading on her horizon like a star sickening towards dawn. Much of the time she felt she lived a meandering monotonous existence, a mind maundering in its sleep with stealthy elusive magnetisms around her. She felt it now as moonily she rolled down a hill towards the unfailing lure of the sea and its tides — sloping down towards a place where her bruised consciousness could sleep towards the thing she called life.

Strange to watch the sea with the rain on it! There were few enough people, most of them fishermen in sou'westers. She was madly tempted to throw off her clothes and swim along those flattened breakers that still rolled shorewards. She was alone among the gulls and the strange piping oyster catchers. She watched a ragged flight of greylag geese going inland. The rain pocked the sea's surface and hissed and smoked on the rollers. The shingle crunched underfoot, scatteringly. All was wildness and wet.

Evening was coming on. The sky in the distance flared smokily through the salt spray, casting a weird yellow shine on the pebbles. She picked one up and examined its firm smooth shape, and the brown skin over flinty black markings. She tossed it underarm into the smooth water before a breaker, saw the brief tiny rings, heard a plop — then it was gone. She imagined the sea — its volume, its depth, its tireless salt strewn depths. God had created great whales — she imagined them surfacing at nightfall, and calling to each other over great distances, harvesting the deep with their great garnering mouths.

There was a body in the sea. She saw it blackened and shiny for a moment among the breakwaters. It brought her heart into her mouth to see it there bobbing and all castaway. She imagined drowning in loneliness, and the thought at last brought tears to her eyes. Then a thin band of mellow sunlight shone through, all smooth and warm on the sea-wracked desolation, and she realised it was a seal. It stuck its head up and she could distinctly see the whiskers before the head went down and brought the body closer to the beach. It plunged and cavorted a short while, then turned bulkily, swam, and she saw it no more.

Her fingers were numb. How white and listless they were. Her hands had been hanging at her side after throwing the pebble. She examined them. They were pinched and white with water and cold, almost as though she could feel the bone growing through. The skin was puckered and — she sucked it — salty. the skin of a land animal. She thought of the cold and the loneliness of the seal: the seal way. Went down to where the breakers boiled white at her feet, bent down and touched the foaming water, almost toppling as it receded fast from her touch.

'Miss Greycliffe!'

There was a voice calling her back to land.

She turned shyly away from the flux of the sea and rain, peering into the gathering gloom. Someone was on the promenade, and was now coming down the steps to the beach. She felt the intrusion personally in her solitude, felt that whoever it was was a kind of trespasser. Felt the wind rushing and soughing, bearing her forward almost as if she were an ungainly gull that should be flying. She felt out of her element, like an albatross.

'Oh Miss Greycliffe!'

It was Mr Hudson.

'Have I found you here, my dear?'

He seemed distraught.

'It's all right,' she called, 'I felt sick at the fair and came down here to collect myself.'

'Thank God I've found you.'

She looked at him smilingly.

'I'm all right.'

'I was afeared when I saw you. I've been combing the fair.'

'You didn't look very far,' she pointed out. 'I saw you when I got off the waltzer.'

'You were with a man.'

'It was only Surtees. He played a trick on me. He told me it would be fun.'

'Wasn't it?'

'No, it was awful.'

'That was a mean trick.'

'I don't think he meant it to be. It was only his idea of having fun.'

'Fun! Will you walk a little? Take my arm?'

She took it, feeling the big friendly warmth.

'You're shivering.'

'I was watching the sea.'

'Ay, dreaming those dreams o' yours no doubt. Miss Greycliffe, I shall never fathom you.'

'There's not much to fathom, I'm afraid. How is Adeline?'

'Well enough. The harvest's a mess.'

'I feared it would be.'

'We must salvage what we can. Look at it out there. Black as pitch.'

They both gazed seaward. The sunlight had disappeared and night was blackening fast. As they gazed the heavens split and a shaft of lightning shivered down onto the distant waves.

She quailed involuntarily. He felt her do so and drew her arm more tightly into his.

'I have to find Surtees and the others. They brought me here.'

'Damn Surtees. I should like to know what he meant by abandoning you here.'

'No he didn't, Mr Hudson. I left him of my own accord. Somehow I've got to find him. They said they would be looking at the lights.'

'The lights stretch for miles.'

There was a distant reverberation of thunder.

'Are you afraid?'

'A little.'

She was like a shell on his arm, so frail he scarcely dared touch her. He wished the thunder and lightning would come and seek them where they stood, for the sheer delight of rushing her up the beach into the town where she would be safe.

'We should walk back.'

'I must stay by the pier. That's where Surtees looked for me before.'

'Damn Surtees,' he said again. 'Can't I drive you, Miss Greycliffe? They wouldn't miss you would they? It would be my pleasure, my particular pleasure.'

'No, Mr Hudson, though I'm very grateful. I should certainly wait.'

'May I wait with you?'

'Of course, if you don't mind the thunder.'

'We should go inland a little. Up the steps on to the promenade. They may be hours yet.'

It was an hour and a half before Surtees arrived, and for one of the two standing there time had flown. The storm came closer and she clung to him. It was nearly overhead. They retreated into a bar, where he bought her bitter lemons while he drank pints. He felt brave as a bull and timid as a kitten. The lights were warm around them. People were laughing and joking while the storm crashed and flickered overhead.

'Surtees will never find you now.'

But he did. He was in the same bar with a group of people from the house, and quite drunk.

'Greycliffe!' he shouted through the noise.

'Miss Greycliffe is with me,' said Mr Hudson.

'Ah, I see she be that, ha ha ha!'

'Mr Hudson found me on the beach.'

'What, still carrying that coconut? Let us all 'ave a piece, Greycliffe.'

She passed it to him. 'Rickcovered from th' waltzer yet?'

'Mr Surtees, that was a mean trick!'

'No, no my chicken, just a liddle bit er old Arthur's fun.'

'Mr Surtees, I warn you to keep a civil tongue in your head when you're with a lady.'

'I'm allus with a leddy. Leddies here, leddies there, Mr Rudson. Seems like you're tewed up wi' a leddy too.'

'That's none o' your business.'

'My business now is to get us all 'ome safe in the dark and the wet. C'me along Greycliffe, we've ben searching fer yer hour after hour, first this way, then that, gettin' wetter and wetter.'

'Oh,' she said, 'in all this storm?'

'Not 'xactly,' he grinned. 'Wetter inside I mean.'

'Are you fit to drive?'

'We sh'll find out. Does your young man require a lift?'

'I've my own car, thank you,' said Mr Hudson stiffly.

'There, there it's only me bit er fun. Well Ronny, the pigeon's roosted at last.'

'So I see.'

'Bit wet about the wings, but otherwise unruffled. The van's just outside, Greycliffe, in Hardgate Street. Listen to that thunder. G'night Mr Rudson.'

'Good night, Miss Greycliffe. Take great care, won't you?'

'I shall,' she promised, leaving him reluctantly.

'C'mon Greycliffe, the storm's gettin' worse,' called Surtees, and she went, waving him a perfunctory goodbye, not dreaming how much indeed her partner's heart was 'tewed up' with her.

IX

Nevertheless their names had been mentioned together. For Mr Hudson it was a delicious secret to hear the rumours. For Elizabeth it was an amusing embarrassment.

More flowers arrived: geraniums this time, in a pot. She put them in her window in the attic.

Then at last a letter from Rex; at least she supposed it was, as she opened it eagerly, noticing the dark curly wave of the postmark and the thick definite writing. It was addressed to Miss E. Greycliffe.

The address inside was London, Brixton.

She imagined him among the yellow houses he must hate. Then the first line. It was a huge disappointment, as if expecting to open her mouth and bite on cake, she bit on air.

Dear Elizabeth,

So cold and formal. She read on in the bitterest disappointment.

I received your letter via your brother. I am sorry to hear that things are proving difficult. I feared they would but felt you were the person to cope with them. Yes it is true I was almost engaged to Miss Hudson but am not any more. I hoped you would not find this out. Does that lower your opinion of me? At the moment things are in a very complicated state and I do not think I can explain them fully. My feelings about you have not changed. I desire to see you every day, and imagine you at work with great clarity. My work is not advancing as I hoped it would. Dear Elizabeth I am in search of the feelings of the people of England. Where are they? What are they? Do the people of England want advertising gimmicks and cheap holidays in the sun? Or do they want to recollect themselves and their natural strengths? I believe the latter. We are not a secular people instinctively but a religious, romantic people. We naturally want large actions, large pillars of faith. To this end I am searching to design a cathedral. They say the age of cathedrals is over. I think this is baloney. They would have us subscribe to Ruskin's decadent notion that the modern cathedrals are all secular buildings — railway stations, and so on. This I deny. I am reading Cobbett. He believes that London and the philosophers and the stockjobbers are all to blame, and that if you ride in the English countryside you see huge churches with no-one in them. This is surely true. How shall we restore the natural rhythms — of seed-time and harvest — to the people? They are all there, waiting to be expressed. We are surely due for a new renaissance — for some new humanism which will go beyond the narrow enthusiasms of chapel-people and the decadent tom-fooleries of imitation. The danger of England today is that it is all to be turned into one gigantic museum, expressive only of vanished glories. Soon you will have to pay £1 admission to look at a ploughed field. Who is doing all this to us? And why do we allow it to happen? Sometimes I think we are overpopulated, and that whereas the surplus population used to be the poor, it has now become the semi-rich and the semi-literate. All the funding and bogus intelligence that goes into advertising! Some remedy is needed — it may be a desperate one.

Believe me, Elizabeth, I did not anticipate that it would be easy, nor that there would be any obvious solutions. The very nature of the life we are encouraged to live today pushes us towards parody — parody of nature, parody of relations too easily labelled class, with all its concomitant violence, parody of accent and dialect, parody of work itself.

I don't want you to go and evangelise the peasants. But feel how close we are still to our vegetable gods. Even supermarkets have a kind of religious substructure. The demons would argue that the supermarket is our modern cathedral. This also I cannot believe. Those large stores express something more than a trade ethic, even with their horrible music, their cut glass, cut price values they still have something potently domestic about them.

I am not going to design a cathedral like a supermarket. Nor am I going to opt for something modernistic like a rocket ship to the almighty. Our aspirations ache out of the ground. We have to begin with the ground and fervour of our being.

Cobbett began with cottage economy. I am asking you to share in a larger version of cottage economy — a country house economy. My aunt suffers from some kind of paralysis. I don't ask you to cure that paralysis, only to observe it and in a way to share it. Too many people today would wish to put her in a rest-home and declare her partially insane. It is my belief that her insanity has some value. So I ask you to continue to leave your degree-insured function as a doctor and to live for a few weeks longer in a woman to woman relationship. Only a few weeks longer! Then surely we shall be free to marry, and after our marriage we can take good care of my aunt together. You and I. It seems like a fairy-tale.

I have to come back to Miss Hudson. Yes, as I have said, I was nearly engaged to her. Why I am not sure. It had something to do with her natural status. She was a daughter of the land — a kind of Flora. You will see what I mean about advertising. The very name has been debased into margarine and keep-fit antics. Fit for what?

Then when I met you I realised I was wrong. Flora was you. (Did you realise that worship of Flora used to include indecent farces?) You are probably unaware of the associations. I want you to remain unaware of the associations. Unashamedly I am, I suppose, using you to discover what will happen when the spirit of Ceres reassumes the land — my aunt is very partial to Pope you know. I want to know you and not to know you. To explain too much would be to ruin you. To explain nothing would no doubt be to ruin you too by making you feel as though you were part of a plot. You are a very special agent. I love you, but have nothing to offer except your own intrinsic vitality.

I can feel I bore you. Most of this must seem like vague mysticism. There are so many gods around seeking for satisfaction. I somehow associate you with the gods of the hedgerow and the sky. Pardon me if I am wrong.

Yours affectionately,
Rex Buckley.

It was the strangest love letter she could imagine. It was such a weird mixture of the abstract, the mechanical and the ethereal. It was a sort of layman's faith. A more satirically minded woman would have sought out occasions for farce and indulged him wickedly with a world like *Cold Comfort Farm*. A more practically minded woman would have thrust the letter into the waste-paper basket and gone in search of home duties. Elizabeth could do neither. She was reminded only of the body of the seal in the vast waters, bobbing and black, whiskery and friendless. She felt intensely lonely.

Flora! So that was how he saw her! He was right, better not to have told her. Yet what he said had its degree of sanity. A poet had said it somewhere: 'the country is the king'. The country would decide when it was sick of the garbage manufactured in its name.

He was in love with an idea, she decided. Still it was a beautiful idea. She imagined him among the waste lots, the building estates, the yards, the groundsel that forced its way up through new sandy paving stones in modern precincts, among arches and echoing courts and advertisement hoardings, timber yards and chimneys, factories with grey corrugated roofs, mock Tudor pubs, walls and warehouses, the lines of cars in parking areas, sodium lights, streets with takeaways and dry cleaners and shops with yellow and red cut price offers, among brick viaducts and canals, orange road cones, concrete motorways, sparkling allotments, deep cuttings and busy junctions; among insurance buildings and office blocks, holding on forlornly to his myth of repudiating the whirl and hullabaloo of the modern world.

Strange to be in love with a man who offered her nothing except herself! A generous offer at any rate. *Nosce teipsum*. She preferred not to know herself.

Instead she stepped out into the air. It was a day for breathing, she decided. There was air everywhere. Great billowing clouds. Mischievous gusts round corners that made you catch at your clothes. Bushes and shrubs did wild dances full of secret glee, then stood with their hands behind their backs like naughty children. It was a day for examining the building more carefully; for observing how this part was Elizabethan, but that section had been built on in the eighteenth century. How weeds grew high up in the gables: yellow bunches of something — ragwort perhaps. It somehow fitted the farrago of a building — a regular hotchpotch of Elizabethan and eighteenth century classical and neneteenth century gothic all stuck together anyhow! She felt flirtatious and funny, in a mood fit for anything. The wind bellied and blustered at her. So she was Flora! Was the wind enacting indecent farces behind her back? How high those clouds tumbled into the sky. Tumbled-up, tumble-down clouds! Such vast spaces intricate with nothingness. A huge laundry of bellying sheets of white.

Well, she had loved him! Well, and she loved him still! That absurd, solemn farce of a letter that had shocked her to the marrow with its coldness when she wanted the warm touch of a friendly hand, a body to clasp to her bosom — that was lovable. Life was like the sea. It looked friendly and yet when you went to cuddle the rollers and join in their whiteness it spat salt at you. She felt wild and irresponsible, wanting to shout with laughter. Flora! Should she go and persecute Mr Hudson's harvest? He was in need of some Flora! She was half-minded to go back to the house and not come out until she had woven a corn dolly. Indeed, that was what she would do! She walked round by the park until she came to the fields. The corn was a sad sight, battered and ravaged, great swathes of it flattened by the wind and rain. There was a kissing-gate nearby. She scrambled through on to a rutted tractor track and began to glean scraps of wind-tossed corn. When she had enough she took it to the side of the path where there was shelter and began to braid and plait the corn into a rudimentary human shape. Gradually it took on a shape as pregnantly boisterous as the day itself. When she had completed it she took it inside and stitched buttons on for eyes. Then, unthinking and exuberant, she sent it with a short note attached to Mr Hudson, wishing him success and profit with his harvest.

The effect on Mr Hudson was galvanic. It was as if it were the sign he had been waiting for. So in a thoughtless moment of exuberance may come the impulse to a deed whose effects are all heartache and bitterness.

It was bound up with a rose. It was the red that caught his eye insistently as he gazed on it in the seclusion of his parlour. To his daughter's repeated questioning as to what it was and where it had come from he returned only a laugh.

'Happen fro' your Mr Buckley,' he said, kicking his heels together at the joke.

'*Mr Buckley?*'

'An' happen not.'

'What *is* it, Father?'

More laughter. 'One o' them there corn-dollies, wishin' us a fertile harvest.'

'Well it must have come from someone.'

'Oh ay, *someone*!'

'Well, who?'

'No idea. It's a joke I 'spect.'

Never was a joke more cherished. The idea of the joke and the idea of the offering became sacramentally entwined. It was incumbent on him to laugh while the dolly was in the house. So long as he laughed they would have a good harvest. So he laughed mightily, with pain in his heart.

His daughter had never seen him like it. Neither had his men. They had come to take his moods for granted when suddenly he was back among them, slapping them on the back with jovial condescension.

'Your missus breeding' agin an' all, Tom Crick?'

'Ay she be allus at it.'

'No fault o' yourn I trow! Must be time o' year. Allus fertile, this time about, choose how. Bulges everywhere. Bigger'en ever, she looks. Ah, Tom 'tis cruel time fer bachelors, th' autumn. Minds yer of times not spent or spent in vain.'

'Yer no bachelor yersen, Mr Rudson.'

'Happen I'm not, yet this time o' year I feel as though I was. Happen I'll be back in the game ere long, who knows.'

'(Believe I know an all)' thought Tom Crick, a mild man with the egg white of his eyes spilling over into the blue and getting mixed up there. '(Appen it's a lass that's behind all this, an if it is I'll lay my wife's forten I know which lass it is an all.)'

'Come Michaelmas, perhaps,' added Mr Hudson self-importantly. 'Sin one o' these ere before, Tom?'

'Why, 'tis a 'arvest queen, all made o' wheat. Now that's a very neat piece er work.'

''Tis that.'

'Which reminds me however, we need a lass for harvest home. We need a vote on that fair soon like. Wonder which it'll be. Young Sarah Lyons, b'chance I reckon.'

'Well you decide on it, Tom. Get the men to place their votes as soon as possible, d'you ear, as soon as possible. Then I shall need help wi'scrumpy for the supper. Make it the biggest harvest home we've ever had, n' darn the expense.'

Left to himself Tom Crick lifted the peak of his flat cap, until he located the bald spot on his cranium and then worried at it with a forefinger.

'Darn the expense,' he articulated slowly. 'Just hear en' darnin' the expense. Must be an especial bit er forten to bring un to that. Darnin' away like 'e owned of the weather and the world. Well, if 'tis she as 'has brought un to darnin' in that kind o' manner, good luck to her an so say all o' us. Darn the expense indeed!'

At other times he was down in the dumps, all savage in temper, egging his men on to greater labours ferociously. At such times there was no way of knowing how to deal with him. Every ditch was a Somme trench to be laboured at under volleys of sarcasm.

'Get into that ditch. Now get out o' that ditch. Now get into that ditch. An' now get out o' that ditch. That way you'll carry more earth on your feet than you ever will all day on th' ruddy spade!'

In the evening he sat and stared at the doll wrapped in its rose. He placed it beside the looking glass where its image doubled on itself. He took the message out of his drawer where he had placed it with the box containing the gold cross, and read it over and over again spelling out the letters as if in capitals until they belaboured his brain.

'This is just to wish you success and profit in your harvest. E. Greycliffe.'

How little it said! Ah, but that was part of the enchantment! The words mesmerised him. They performed strange antics. He put them in front of the mirror like a charm, and allowed himself the luxury of reading them backwards.

He picked the lilac paper up and sniffed it, sure that he could smell her entrancingly elusive perfume on the page. Once he got some tracing paper and traced, with infinite care, his tongue protruding an inch from his lips, the rare outline of her script. How fine it was. After a while he became sure that he could see her face in the paper behind the words, as if dissolving into lips. He kissed them fervently.

It was, somehow, the idea of the woman's hand lying so gracefully and negligently across the page as she penned the lines that attracted him most. He felt sure he could identify the neat shape of her wrist bone in the curve of the letters, and could imagine the curve of her own lips following the word, as though she had blown them into life with the effortful grace of a glassblower.

Even when the light was out he lay sleepless in his bed, watching how the moon came up and silvered the glass. The rose was now pure black like a funeral seal. He got up and lit a pipe and sat there before the table, alternately smoking and allowing the words to etch themselves into his mind. Now he took the cross out of its box and hung it round the neck of the wheaten doll. He was tempted to write a note in return, switched the light on, rummaged for paper, found none, tramped downstairs to the kitchen at the dead of night, returned with some calendar paper. He was unused to writing, and as he did so curls of tobacco from his pipe fell on the page, casting hot tracks and singe marks. Nevertheless he accomplished a note of a kind:

Dearest Miss Greycliffe, I know your name is Elizabeth but dare not call you by it yet. Soon I shall have earned the right to no doubt I hope. We have never had so big a harvest. It is a kind of miracle, of your disposing. I enclose a cross. I bought it for your birthday but never dared give it to you then. I have kept it safe and sound ever since in my big chest of drawers upstairs in my bedroom. Nobody knows about it, and if you so will, nobody need know about it for it is small enough to lie all invisible about your lovely neck, only known about by us two. Will you be mine? That is to say as plain as possible, will you marry me? I have no hope of ever satisfying all your beauty and all your queenly qualities but I do love you so. There! I have said it now and darn all the consequences.

Yours ever,
Roger Hudson

It was the longest letter he had ever written. He folded it very carefully into four and laid it alongside the box containing the cross. This drawer he began to consider her wedding trousseau. Gradually he accumulated a small pile of gifts. He had a record downstairs of his favourite music, *The Dream of Olwen*, on an old seventy-eight, bought for his former wife. It was his most cherished sentimental possession. He placed it in the drawer. He began to wonder about the kind of clothes she wore, and was to be seen in a store in town fingering perfumes and chiffon scarves. He bought a scarf of silvery blue which he considered suited her fine, and also some perfume called *Aimée* which had, to his unpractised nose, a most subtle and refined aroma. He began to imagine that he was married and would sometimes set aside the best portions of his breakfast on a separate plate, leaving them uneaten.

To Adeline his behaviour was inexplicable. It was as though he were sickening in some way. He seemed to be turning into two people. One was the irrepressibly hale farmer whose life was a business, the other was a subtle and shy other person who spoke in a whisper, who had bags under his eyes from sleepless nights, and who did increasingly furtive and eccentric things seemingly behind his own back. She began to wonder if he was sickening for one of those modern illnesses of the mind. Schizophrenia! She felt very proud when the name came unbidden to her memory. Her father was behaving as if he were schizophrenic. She wondered whether she should call a doctor.

For Mr Hudson the most urgent thing possible was for him to discover the occasion for and to perform some deed of derring-do. Having settled the fact with his conscience that he was in love the next thing was some sublime action on her behalf. Remembering the gentle quailing under the threat of a thunderstorm he began to pray for the worst possible weather, getting into leonine rages when the unsettled climate turned obdurately beneficent. At no point did he consider allowing his daughter into the secret. She would mock him, he was certain. Somehow he had to erupt into the heart of the girl he loved. He walked around like an unexploded mine.

By day he stopped on his tractor to consider the greeny golden and silky white acres that were his, moving under steep-cloud-banked skies. Imagined gathering all the grains together and presenting it in the greatest bouquet ever seen. The clouds massed and piled but though occasionally they rained they never thundered. He drove his tractor through the fields and down deep lanes leading to sunlight with his mind fixed on her, and the steadily accumulating treasure-trove in his drawer. Every facet of rained-on sunlight was another jewel in the necklaces of desire. Necklace! The very word filled him with new emotions, as he imagined the fine gold lace around her throat, the gold cross nestling securely between breasts that even his wildest most masculine fantasies did not permit him to uncover to the eyes of his mind. She was the fields he drove across, was the harvest and all the hallows of a sunlit festival. She was flags and bunting; and every day was a royal progress for him towards an idea so diffuse and vaguely impassioned as to be a huge serene horizon of achievement.

X

'I am in a sense the harvest, you see,' said Miss Oldcastle.

Elizabeth did not see, but a pin was insecurely placed and all her energies were concentrated on securing it in safety, both to herself and the owner.

'Without my presence in the scene the scene would die. After all, what do they care, those old farmers and reprobates? No romance. No imagination. Harvest! Why, the very word would die. It's a very picturesque word, wouldn't you agree? I wonder what its derivation is. Old English, I expect. The time of reaping and gathering. Richness and fruitition. People think old age is sad. I'm laughing! Whoops. Hoorah! Hoorah for the harvest. A billion years of evolution comes to this — an old miss in her rocking chair rotting at the beam-ends of her desires.

Do you have desires, Greycliffe? I'm sure you're far too sensible. A lot of rot is talked about spring. Bah, there's no such thing as spring. It's all either delayed winter or delayed summer. Usually the former. I detest spring. Where's the poetry of springtime? A few seeds here and there, a daffodil perhaps; no sir, springtime gives me the willies.

Whereas autumn. Ah, autumn indeed. No willies there. Even the rain's warm. What's the matter, Greycliffe? Fingers like thumbs and you're about to sneeze — don't deny it, I felt a tremor. Sneezes are for spring. Hay fever you know. That's all I ever see: men and women with red streaming eyes and a pout of dissatisfaction. People expect so much. Have you ever known people satisfied? Funny if the year stopped at autumn. If things just went on getting bigger and fatter until they burst. Like a joke, you know. The kind of joke that's too big to see. I once saw a cartoon — well that was in the days when I had eyes to see — and read, you know. All those books downstairs.

I read them once. In my hayday I was a great reader. I don't know where it's all gone, can scarcely remember a line or a rhyme now. Sclerosis, that's the word. Arterial sclerosis in the poetry glands. My glands are horribly dry. Stop pushing that pin around, it may puncture something.

This cartoon, there were two travellers, in a foreign land. They stood in the giant footprints of some abominable monster. The yeti, I expect. They'd probably pursued it for years. One looked at the other pushing back his hat and said, "I see no sign of it". That's a joke. Just like the autumn. A multitudinous time of year. Braid my hair if you please — or no, stop, *plait* it rather.'

Elizabeth plaited dutifully. Miss Oldcastle did indeed begin to look like the corn dolly. She considered sending her to Mr Hudson as an additional gift.

'What are you smiling at, Greycliffe?'

'I was not, Miss Oldcastle, I . . .'

'Oh yes you were. I felt a smile dig right down into your finger tips. Is it my hair? Funny stuff, hair. You wonder what it's there for half the time. Now if we were all bald wouldn't that be strange? A mere fetish half the time. Maids must have hair or men wouldn't woo. Woo: a peculiar word. It reminds me of pigeons. Wood pigeons. Mad you know; completely. Hypocrites! That's right — get both your hands working. Dig, dig, dig!

What do you do in harvest, Greycliffe? Stop, that's an unfair question. Is there any truth in the rumour that you're having an affair with farmer Hudson? And my nephew? Well, you must be a busy lady. Yet you look as slim as aspens. Let's have a look at you. See how you're getting on. Come out from behind my back. Stand there. That's right. As if for a photograph. I wish I were a camera. Wouldn't I just burrow into you. With my folding snout, and buttons for eyes. Stand there, Greycliffe. Oh, she's a feast for my wretched eyeballs. They say I need a bailiff, did you know that? Land's going to wrack and ruin around me.'

Miss Oldcastle sat with her back to the sun, looking as if aflame. Elizabeth stood in front of her.

Miss Oldcastle planted a kiss on the full lips.

'That's better. I want to eat my fill of you. Devour you with my cormorant eyes. Never saw such a picture of health and beauty. Very dangerous substances. They ignite, you know. Wonder if they've ignited my nephew. He's like touchwood. Tinder wood. Strikes easily. Wonder where he's burning now? We all wonder that Greycliffe, not just you. But you wonder it particularly, don't you? Hah! All smiles stopped together. You won't know who wrote that will you?'

'No, Miss Oldcastle.'

'Robert Browning, of course. God knows what he meant. That was his joke. "When I wrote that only God and Robert Browning knew what it meant. Now only God knows." I think I know what he meant, Greycliffe. Funny how your eyes never smile. Wonder why not. "When Irish eyes are smiling . . ." put some elbow grease into it girl, or we'll be here all day. No company today. Just myself. Do you know what happens when I take dinner with myself? "No Miss Oldcastle". Well I'll tell you. I take dinner with a huge mirror opposite me. A convex mirror. It makes the room look tiny, but makes me look huge. HUGE. Like the old woman in Dickens, face in a tablespoon. I like to watch myself eating. *Enfin* . . . that's very nice — for once! Don't let it go to your head. I should like to see you in plaits. Very Aryan you'd look — now that's a wicked word, isn't it? We don't like that word in our class-room, do we? Are you a teacher, Greycliffe?'

'No, Miss Oldcastle.'

'No, I never accused you. That's my last duchess — who was his first, eh? Ah well, we shall never know. We aren't *intended* to know. You know, I fancy you as a duchess, Greycliffe — or rather as a baroness. Morganatic. That means you only get the morning gift. No property. Would leave you very *morne*, wouldn't it? *Très triste alors! Pardieu! Bonté divine!* All dismal and dreary. Greycliffe's occupation's gone. When I say they, I mean *them*. All of them. You should hear the walls resound. As though a million stick insects had gone berserk. Gossip, gossip, gossip. They're full of speculation. Well, I speculate a little. That's why I like to look in the mirror. The walls in this house are very thin.'

'I thought they were rather thick, Miss Oldcastle.'

'You thought! I wonder what you *do* think. Whether you do think. Do you think you're mad?'

'No, Miss Oldcastle.'

'Not likely. Not yet. You will do. We're all mad here. Playing blind man's buff. Hand me the razors. No, take them back again, the time's not yet come. Did you know that it was an almost universal habit with people when leaving a bank to carefully adjust their pockets if they have been receiving money? I watch them all the time. No money comes into this house without my knowledge. Do you think I'm very rich?'

'I scarcely know.'

'You scarcely care you mean. Well, you must be made to care. I'm your property, you see. Do you see that?'

'In a way I see that.'

'It's comparatively obvious. You're playing with your hands again, girl. Come read to me. Read me some real poetry. None of that morbid mopy stuff you read the other day. Tickle my fancy. "Ye Gods! Annihilate but space and time, And make two lovers happy".'

She shook with laughter. 'What a festival it'd be. Autumn when the pheasant whirrs. We have pheasants, I expect you've seen them.'

'Yes, Miss Oldcastle.'

'Don't they whirr and clack: don't they just? Like knitting machines. We used to have peacocks but I ate 'em. Every one. Nasty noisy birds. Kraarck! Screech! Horrible noise. Vain things, birds. Vain and brainless. Always laying eggs. I'd ban 'em their boxes. A brain of feathers and a heart of lead. Fine definition. Come, hand me my Pope. A Catholic you know. Well, I'm no Catholic. Don't have much religion hereabouts. Have you met the vicar?'

'No, Miss Oldcastle.'

'Mr Warburton. Very nice name. Very nice man. Oh, you'd trap the vicar mi'lady. One glance from those dusky eyelids and he'd be a goner. That's why I keep you apart. No place for you at *my* revels.

> Vital spark of heav'nly flame!
> Quit, oh quit this mortal frame:
> Trembling, hoping, ling'ring, flying,
> Oh the pain, the bliss of dying.

Very apt sentiment. That's how we all feel no doubt. At least we should. Don't hear much trembling, hoping, etcetera downstairs, not in that cause at any rate. Trembling, hoping, ling'ring, flying.

Oh the pain, the bliss of *her upstairs* a-dying — that's what they all think, without thinking what'd become of 'em all. Well, I'll tell you. What about *you* Greycliffe?'

'Me, Miss Oldcastle?'

'Yes you madam. In my place. Wouldn't that be a neat little poem? How Miss Oldcastle died — ugh, horrible word — quitted this life in bliss — and left the house and all its appurtenances to her *maid*! That'd bring the peacocks back. Kraarck! Screech! Left her everything. And my nephew to be appointed steward. After many years of ungainly courtship they married and lived happily ever after. Isn't that the perfect little poem? Eh, Greycliffe? Wouldn't that suit you very nicely? Well, it shan't happen. I'm not quitting this mortal frame *just* yet, even though it creaks abominably. Not for you nor for him nor for them either; come read to me a little, make me laugh!'

Elizabeth read as she was directed, and though the lines seemed arid and self-centred, Miss Oldcastle cackled with shrewd laughter.

'I've a pigmy frame but a big bosom, Greycliffe. "This long disease my life" — how it makes me laugh. Do you know how high he was, the little Queen Anne's man? Four foot nothing. All that poetry squeezed into that little crippled carcase. Do you know how high I am?'

'No, Miss Oldcastle.'

'There, there nobody does. Because when I'm with my mirror I'm huge. There, measure me.'

'Here? Now?'

'Here and now. Take that tape measure. Now I'll stand against the wall. Get a pencil!'

It was a tricky business measuring the old woman for she felt, to Elizabeth's fingers, like a rag and bone doll. Her arms were pitifully thin.

'Measure me, I say.'

Elizabeth measured carefully.

'The right height appears to be four foot five and a half inches,' she reported.

'That'll fix 'em. Every day they want to measure me. Do you know why?'

'No, Miss Oldcastle.'

'They want to measure me for my coffin, that's why. This'll settle 'em. Every day I want you to measure me, and every day

I'll grow a little. I'm the Queen of this castle you know. They shan't fix me so easy. I'll unsettle their plans. I'll grow. Bigger and bigger. They'll burst when they see me.

> Peeled, patched, and piebald, linsey wolsey brothers
> Grave murmers! Sleeveless some, and shirtless others.

That'll fix 'em.'

'Miss Oldcastle, you shouldn't hate everybody so much. I'm sure . . .'

'Oh ay, you're sure, are you? Are you certain you're sure? Besides, why shouldn't I hate 'em? It keeps me alive, hating everybody so much. Keeps me going through autumn. Oh, I know their fickle, sickle-faced joys, their "God bless Miss Oldcastle" — I *know* 'em, you see. Now I'll let you go gently off to your pleasures, though God knows where you find them in this God forsaken vicinity. Call the maid. No, ring the bell — good heavens, girl, do I still have to tell you?'

Elizabeth rang the bell but was yet detained.

They call it autumn but to me it is winter. Did you feel the cold just then?'

'No, madam.'

'A sword of cold passed through my body. Now I wonder what *that* portends.'

'It is chilly — chillier than it was. The leaves are beginning to rot.'

'Rot! I should say they are. Saturated, aren't they? Ah Bastuble, the time has come the walrus said. Shall we have oysters tonight? Nice, sweet, delectable finely bearded Whitstable oysters with beef and beer?'

'No, ma'am.'

'What, not tonight? Well, when shall we? Never, I surmise. Give me the menu, let's see, let's see. Potatoes and roast pork. Well, some nice juicy crackling. I still have my teeth you see, Greycliffe. Gnashers I call 'em. Much weeping, wailing and gnashing of teeth there'll be when I snuff it, won't there, girl?'

'Yes, madam.'

'Yes, madam. Thank you kindly, madam. Did you leave me a millionairess, madam, so's I can marry my nice young man? Have you *got* a nice young man, Bastuble?'

'Fairly, ma'am.'

'Well that's it. You see, Greycliffe. (Oh lor' madam not before the other maids.) The other maids are all the same. What was that you said about the leaves. *Rotting?* Well let 'em rot. Let 'em rot right down into compost and so the whole cycle begins again. Stupid, don't you think? Years being circular and that? At my age they are. No sooner begun than you're rolling off the other side. Not like when you're young. Years are any shaped but mainly rectangular with a nice point aimed at Christmas and the New Year. And another, you all say, and another. What is it, this morganatic morning gift? Oh, I didn't tell you? Shall I shock you badly? It's the gift made by the husband on the morning after the consummation of the marriage. A bitter thought. Mine 'ud give me pease pudding and black bread, no doubt. Pork with crackling! What a consummation. What about the poor little piggy-wiggy, weeping fat through his bloated little eyes? Tears of fat. That just about sums it all up. Never mind, never mind, they're all the same, Greycliffe. There, you may take me Bastuble, but gently mind, ever so gently, I'm a toy you know in your great red capable hands.'

She went, leaving Elizabeth brain sick and baffled, looking out of the window on to the lawn below. The leaves were indeed rotting silently into leaf mould. Silently? She opened the window. The wind tugged at her sleeve, but even so she was sure that below the sound she could hear the faint hiss and trepidation of the leaves falling and preparing to fall in their green and yellow glory.

She found herself in the garden, walled, with red brick softened by sunlight, with oast houses overlooking it, and a meadow beyond on which a long level evening light fell, steeping itself in swathes of grass and tufts of thistle. In spring there would be darker tangles of bluebells clumped in juicy bundles. There were overarching boughs — a world of wood and water, for the stream could be clearly heard, belling and clucking somewhere beyond in the wood itself.

The grass was already wet, soaking her shoes, dampening on her long skirt, as she walked among the paths and neglected mess of vegetation at the bottom, down towards the ditch which was full of dark, muddy water, glutted with snails and floating scum. The trees overhung here, and she walked in blue shadows, looking up, sunblind, askance, as the light streamed through into her hair, in beams of pale gold, darkening her fairness as light will darken on silver.

Behind her she could hear voices in the house, laughter, a cleared throat, and someone singing; it was all going on in its way, in a way that she did not really understand. They were as foreign in their peculiar kindness as she was, she supposed, to them in her solitariness.

The light was already fading. It softened and gathered thick shadows around it. A snail shell crunched underfoot, and a clump of nettles swiped viciously at her unstockinged calf. The garden was pitted with holes, and she preferred to imagine foxes and wild things living there, moving delicately and tremulously among them.

Evening came on, dove grey everywhere, soft and faded. It was *Der Abschied* — the year's leavetaking. The earth seemed to ache for some deliverance. What was the word Miss Oldcastle had used? *Morne*, yes, it was *morne*. The beautiful French word fell like petals among the arbours and parterres of the house and its courtyards. Mankind's relation with the earth was so arduous and so easily spoiled. Either he raped it with efficiency and machines or he patted it into gardens that were oh so neat and pretty and yet so stifling to larger movements of the spirit. There! She was thinking like Rex after all. She imagined his spirit, moving dissatisfied and restless amidst all the intricate regularities of his aunt's rule. For make no mistake: Miss Oldcastle *did* rule. Someone kept the gardens neat under her persuasion.

Further down there were tennis courts. She moved towards them, imagining white figures at play. Would she be pleased to see them or not? Figures like moths at curfew tide, when all the land was dew-fallen. She imagined the ghosts of voices — 'Play up, and play the game!' — of children lurking in the bushes in ambush like red indians, laughing and eager. No, there were no children here, no room for children.

A heron flew overhead, like the one she had seen at Eastminster, all tipped with gold. She imagined the little seaside town on such an autumn evening, with the tide out and the holes of lugworms puddling the mud flats, and fishing boats on their beam ends. It was the year's turning — the fall they used to call it — when the earth brought forth strange baptisms of beauty out of its own grief and inconsolable losses. Such richness, such fertility, all to die — and in dying to be reborn; in dying *being* reborn.

The tennis courts were a wilderness, all forlorn, all, all forlorn! She scarcely knew whether she would welcome their rebirth. For suppose there were children, and a vicarage tea-party, the clunk of croquet, and white-garmented figures strolling here and there — the smell of a pipe, the soft smoke going up from those geometrically insane chimneys at the house. Would she feel any happier? No, she decided she would not. It was better so, to see how the ivy entwined the nets of the courts and how rust made the wire netting vivid as leaves. Such ruin everywhere. Fall and decay in everything, fall and decay.

And yet she wanted to dance. Silently among the unwatching trees she shaped the movements of waltz to herself, her face flushing to the quick magic of the three beats. Strange sad music, always in waltzes in spite of the quick time. Over the beat there was always laid, inlaid, those fervent bold, sad, melodies. *The Blue Danube. The Emperor.* She danced the *Emperor*, feeling its music burgeon round her like late butterflies. She danced with tentativeness and trepidation, turning the swish of leaves into music around her, the music of the earth and music of men of the earth blending insensibly one into the other. The trees brushed her ears like strings, the unheard birds were lamenting like a cor anglais. All was music, but her heart was not of it, her heart was sad in ways that no music could reach or express.

Yes, the earth ached for deliverance, but from what or how she could not determine. Moods touched her fleetingly — some stern and peremptory, some of admonishment, some meltingly angelic, — and left her entranced but as if blind, feeling her way through a myriad ways.

She walked on, away from the tennis courts into a maze. It made her laugh at first, thinking of the maze in *Three Men in a Boat*, and Harris leading the way. But there were no bobbing heads here, no fat men with red faces, only the suffocation of the dead green yew hedges, all clipped and fine, but unyielding and harsh in their weird symmetry. The ground underfoot was reddish brown. Once she thought she saw a snake, but it proved only to be a dead twig.

The centre of the maze was a place of stillness, unnatural order and silence. There was a blue peeling wooden seat with a scattering of yellow leaves blown from some other part of the garden. She sat down a moment, burying her face in her hands.

Her heart was calling, calling, with strange notes that would be translated neither into speech nor into thought.

A bird was singing insistently. A robin or a wren — that spilling brilliance of song which was its own death song. All so keen yet so lonely, pointing up the silence around of the unruffled hedges.

It struck her that she had reached the centre of the maze unimpeded, as if in a trance. Rising, she turned out into the alleys and was immediately lost. The wind must have changed, or perhaps her attitude, for she could now hear, infuriatingly close, sounds from the offices and the workshops — hammering, someone whistling — yet every time she pursued these noises she found herself at a dead end. It began to irk her, meeting wall after wall, her arms plucked at by the yew hedges; destroyed the mood of trance and abandonment which had brought her to the spot, was like the plot — if that was what it was — which entangled her, full of awkward turns and no obvious continuations. Suddenly she had been translated from a free thing moving, however helplessly, in its own music, into a game of chess. She could imagine people observing her — looked up at the big blind windows of the house as if expecting to see faces at the windows, laughing and applauding their own cleverness. They could pick her up and set her down at will. Her imprisonment was their liberty. Her mind was plucked at by these thoughts, and reverberated angrily. The sense of being known yet not knowing — well that was universal, but when the knowledge was in the minds of people rather than chance or the elements, then you felt the suffocation of a trap. She did not want to be known, or to know. It was like a trance turning into a dream, a dream where you were playing some part in a play whose dimensions were unseen by you, where the other characters were unknown, and where at any moment it was obscure whether you were walking the stage or fumbling about in the wings. It was not that she required to be central to life — had very little desire to be a *prima donna* — but only that she required to have some centrality to her own experience of life; to have it allowed to herself that these moods, sometimes fickle enough, signified something, and were not to be disallowed her in the name of some other sport to be declared during her absence.

The idea of a sport thickened around her. It was going dark

in earnest, and still no way out. If they were in some way hunting her. Not a game at all but a blood sport. She was a quarry — seemingly in both senses of the word, for if animals were being used around her they were digging into her tooth and nail.

These were morbid thoughts. It was with something of a shock that she came out eventually into clear air and the end of the day to find the house facing her serene and mellow, like a great forehead bathed in the last of the light. The dying of the light. The moon was already up, riding misty and rich-coloured through terraces of cloud, dyeing the sky around it, but leaving the blue of the distance more intensely blue and silver than ever. Ragged clouds lay in the yellow west. All was still, all was quiet, save the short bark of fox, and the strange churning cry of a nightjar. She returned indoors, not unperplexed, but in a way resolved as if into components and particles of peace; in exile, but at home with herself, lonely but free.

XI

> Ah! see her hovering feet
> More bluely veined, more soft, more whitely sweet
> Than those of sea-born Venus, when she rose
> From out her cradle shell.

Thus would Mr Hudson have thought had he been able to conceive in the medium of the highest utterance. As he could not, he continued to buy anything that took his fancy. The drawer began to creak and groan under the weight of accumulated stuff — scarves, petticoats, stockings, woollens, perfumes, all gathered into one great granary and there allowed to lie as if burgeoning. The centre of it all remained the cross and the letter, and the letter which was the cause of it all with its now fading rose.

The harvest was well-nigh finished — all was safely gathered in, except for the greatest prize of all. The queen of the harvest, who was Sarah Lyons, as predicted, had played her part prettily, but not prettily enough to conjure the farmer's eyes out of the vacant air, where he saw a dress similar enough in shape to Sarah's but with a different figure in it.

The shape of his darling was visibly present at the harvest supper for she was invited, and sat professing herself delighted through all the speeches and songs and the huge supper itself. She sat next to Adeline, a neat and comely figure in porcelain, but Elizabeth was sculpted air and swan down to the farmer's heated imagination. His eyes lowered at her whenever she was offered a drink; and he drank covertly with her, mouthful by mouthful.

During the supper he had the idea of his life. To lure the lady by means of his daughter on an unexpectedly dangerous walk, from which he, Roger Hudson, would save them in a way that would exhibit all the nerve and virility he possessed. It would be done — but ah, that was the secret, how it would be done. Afterwards, she might accept. The fact that he had notions of reading about the idea in a book long ago stirred his imagination as a poker stirs fire. That would show her he was no clod, no yokel, but a literary man in his ways, if she could conjecture such a thing as a solid pun. This one would be very solid.

'How father prods at one, when there's something in the wind,' said Adeline to Elizabeth one day soon after the supper.

'Why,' answered Elizabeth laughing, 'what's in the wind?'

They were baking bread together at the big farmyard kitchen table; a square-legged antique in deal and oak with thick-ribbed grain now covered in flour and lakes of lukewarm water which the girls puddled as if building sandcastles.

'A walk's in the wind, that's what,' retorted Adeline, 'a walk up Coldharbour Lane way.'

'Well, shall we do it? Is it very special?'

'It's nothing special, that's what's so puzzling. Nothing but a few fields and a barn or two. The other way, that leads to the village is much prettier, but that isn't what he wants us to do.'

'So shall we go to please him? Or would you rather we went the other way?'

'I'd much rather go the other way, but it's in his head we should go his way. That's what I mean about him prodding. "Eh Addie, won't you walk up Coldharbour way in a bit with Miss Elizabeth?" He keeps on at me, cracking his joints and looking mysterious. I guess he wants to get on with something special at the house but I can't imagine what.'

'Since that's what he wants we'll do it — this afternoon, if you like.'

'I do like. I love walking anywhere around your farm. It feels so much freer than at the house.

'Well, we'll go then. There, set the dough like that in the tins for it to rise. I'll just cover it with a warm cloth and put it here by the range. That's right. Make sure the cloth is nice and damp. Mmm! I love the smell when it's all quaggy and rough like that.'

The dough was set aside and hats and coats were brought from the hall.

Coldharbour Lane was narrow and twisty, sunk amidst walls

of chalk, but gradually, as the girls walked, it rose uphill and began to command some not very spectacular views of grazing land. The hills were not steep enough to give any sight of the sea, though the bleached hills beyond had that curious soft numinousness around their escarpments that tells of sea air and visionary blue distances. The girls were about a mile from the farm and deep in conversation — at least Adeline was — about the nature and price of rings — when they were diverted from their chat by a new and unwelcome arrival in their field of vision.

About two hundred yards away there was a track that led from pasture land down to the road they were walking along, and standing on the track, gazing at them doubtfully, was a cow that had got loose from its field.

Elizabeth paid it scant attention but Adeline looked closer, and pulled her by the arm. 'That bull shouldn't be out.'

'Bull,' said Elizabeth curiously, 'I thought it was only a cow.'

While they stood in doubt, the animal decided to clarify matters by coming towards them. It was a large specimen of the breed, reddish dun in colour, though somewhat disfigured at present by splotches of mud about his sides. His horns were thick and tipped with brass. Between his nostrils and through the gristle of his nose was a stout copper ring, welded on, and to the ring was attached an ash staff about a yard long, which the bull, with the motions of his head, flung about like a flail. It was not till they observed this dangling stick that the young women were really alarmed; for it revealed that the bull was an old one, too savage to be driven, which had in some way escaped, the staff being the means by which the driver controlled him and kept his horns at arm's length.

'I know him,' gasped Adeline, '"tis Jonas, father's old Jersey bull. Oh, he's terribly savage! What shall we do? Which way shall we go? It would be dangerous to run.'

They looked round for some shelter or hiding place, and thought of the barn nearby. As long as they had kept their eyes on the bull he had shown some deference in his manner of approach; but no sooner did they turn their backs to seek the barn than he tossed his head, and decidedly to thoroughly terrify them. This caused the two girls to run wildly, whereupon the bull advanced in a deliberate charge.

The barn stood behind a green slimy pond, and it was closed except for one of the usual pair of doors facing them, which had been propped open by a hurdle stake, and for this opening they made. The interior had been cleared by a recent bout of threshing, except at the end, where there was a stack of dry clover. Adeline took in the situation. 'We must climb up there,' she said.

But before they had even approached it they heard the bull scampering through the pond without, and in a second he dashed into the barn, knocking down the hurdle-stake in passing. The heavy door slammed behind him, and all three were imprisoned together. The bull saw them and stalked towards the end of the barn into which they had fled. The girls doubled so adroitly that their pursuer was against the wall when the fugitives were already half way to the other end. By the time that his length would allow him to turn and follow them they had crossed over; and so for a few minutes the pursuit continued. What might have happened had their situation continued cannot be said; but in a few moments a rattling of the door distracted their fearsome adversary's attention, and a man appeared. He ran towards the leading staff, seized it, and wrenched the animal's head as if he would snap it off. The wrench was so violent that the thick neck seemed to have lost its stiffness and to become half-paralysed, whilst the nose dropped blood.

The man was seen in the partial gloom to be large-framed and unhesitating. He led the bull to the door, and the light revealed Mr Hudson. He made the bull fast without, and re-entered to help the ladies. It would have been gratifying if Elizabeth had clung to him and cried, 'You — have saved me'. In fact she did something equally gratifying to his enraged senses, for she fainted in his arms.

He picked her up tenderly and carried her to the clover-heap, and waited until she opened her eyes in the gloom. Then she did ask.

'How — comes it to be you — you?'

'I followed you here. They told me at the farm this is the way you'd have gone.'

'How lucky! And Adeline ... Is she ...?'

'She's safe!' cried Adeline. 'Oh Father, you must have *known*!'

'I know? Not I. Not that that dangerous creature was on the rampage. How could I have known? Now, Miss Elizabeth, no harm can come to you now, my dear, my dear one.'

The words came strangely to her through her thickened

consciousness; it was as though she were hearing voices under water.

'All those hints. You deliberately led us into danger.'

'Do you think I'd have allowed old Jonas to harm a hair on your head? No, think again, Addie, the old scaramouche must have found his own way out of the field, but it was lucky I was passing by.'

Yet he had done it. And he exulted in the knowledge, just as he exulted in the weight of the fair form that had lain momentarily in his arms.

Mr Hudson supporting Elizabeth on one side, and Adeline on the other, they went slowly along the lane together. They were about to descend towards the farm when Adeline remembered that she had left her hat in the barn.

'I'll run back,' she said. 'I don't mind at all. I'm not as exhausted as you are.' She thereupon hurried back, the others pushing on their way.

Elizabeth was still only half-recovered and was pressing hard on the farmer's arms. It seemed natural for him to put his arm round her waist and keep it there until they arrived at the house.

There, all was fuss. A bath was immediately prepared, and a bed too, 'for Miss Elizabeth had been taken unwell.'

The invalid found herself being cossetted from all directions. A new pearl-grey nightdress miraculously discovered itself as she soaped and drenched herself in foamy unguents. But strangest of all was to find herself lying in her bed, studying the letter which Mr Hudson had at last brought himself to deliver, and holding in her hands a chastely beautiful cross of gold.

XII

It was all too much to cope with. She scarcely knew whether to laugh or cry as she studied the careful script. 'I know your name is Elizabeth but dare not call you by it yet.'

Well, he had now. As they walked back from the barn he had pressed her close to his side, articulating the new name as though it were foreign. To discover herself again from a new angle. He wanted her passionately, had endeavoured to kiss her with kisses as dry as chalk. It was in vain that she had tried to explain her predicament, he would not listen. He was self-glorified in some way. He teased and cajoled her: 'just a liddle old bull' — but the terror of the encounter was still on her and she flinched from all references to the event, and could feel, even through the drowsiness of her swoon, that the flinching was delicious to him.

Indeed it was. The event was more delectable than he could have dared to hope. He radiated masculinity. The earth element moved in him and made him feel god-like, along with some truculence and a sense of retribution. Hadn't she gored him on the horns of desire? Hadn't she tossed and sported with his heart until he felt it was made of hay? He was irresistible in his advances. Hadn't she seen it, hadn't she felt it. It was fatal. It was called destiny. He was triumphant and looked down at her with an elephantine sense of exuberant privilege; reared above her with weird and unspeakable tenderness.

Adeline returned and for a while some sense of order returned with her. Adeline was quickly able to make sense of what had happened, scolded her father for submitting them to such danger, and explained the situation to her friend.

'It's just one of Dad's stupid infatuations. He gets like it occasionally. It'll wear off but you'll have to put up with it for a while.' Then, more petulantly, 'I don't want you for my mother, I want you for my friend.'

The idea of being a mother! Things were out of control.

'I don't want to be your mother,' said Elizabeth faintly.

This was worse than useless.

'Then why did you cajole him so? You must have said something to him. He wouldn't act like this unless there were particular reasons.'

Suddenly she was on the defiant side of things.

'You ought to marry him. Indeed you should. I won't have anybody contampering with my father's affections. You owe it to him now. He saved your life.'

'You said he didn't ...'

'He did, he did! Don't listen to what I say, act on your heart, Elizabeth. Weren't you glad to see him.'

'Yes of course, but ...'

'Because nobody can handle a bull like him. It made me proud to see him. None of the hands would dare tackle Jonas in that mood.'

'Thank God it wasn't a hand.'

'There you are you see, you praise him.'

'Adeline I cannot marry him, I'm already promised ... there, I've told you.'

'Promises are made to be broken. The world's one great broken promise. Take him, Elizabeth, or he'll kill you and then he'll kill himself. He isn't in control any more.'

'Neither am I.'

'You love him. You made him love you .'

'I ... did not.'

'That ring on your finger ...'

'Which ring?'

'That one.'

It was true. He must have slipped it on while she was fainting. The sense of being possessed was like a nightmare.

Later he came and sat with her. She tried to laugh it off.

'I was very silly. I acted very foolishly.'

'You needed me. I saw it immediately.'

He held her hand. Even now she was grateful for that, for it made her feel like a child in trouble. If only he were her father. For that was what she most needed: counsel and warmth. She was tossed on a black sea and saw blackness before her eyes again.

'There, there, my dearest, you'll soon be well.'

She had gone very white. He fingered the ring. She felt him exploring her hand like a trophy.

'Mr Hudson ...'

'Roger, my dear one. Oh, Elizabeth, if you knew what pain you've caused me, how I have waited.'

'What caused it?'

This was a delicious proposition to consider. He looked down at the hand with the ring, the pinkish grey, slightly blunt, oddly practical fingers, and decided that was not it. He looked at her body, only partly covered by the sheet, the bosom heaving with unrest, and decided that was not it. He looked at her pale lips slightly parted, and kissed them. She turned away. Roughly, and with considerable tenderness he pulled her face towards his and kissed it again. She could feel the stubble of his chin and smell the strange incense of tobacco, but felt no other sensations.

'Oh my dear,' he groaned, dandling her hand covetously.

'It was in the writing, o' course.'

He repeated, as though a lesson had been learned, the words of her letter. But otherwise words failed him. Words had no place here. She was decidedly his. He had decided. When he saw her, he said to himself, 'That's her'; when he touched her, he said to himself, 'That's it'. Nothing could come between him and his infatuation.

She slept a little and woke to find him still sitting there. There was an alteration in the room. It was full of clothes.

'They're for you, my dear one. I bought them all, every one.'

'Oh, Roger ...'

'That's what I love to hear. Say my name over and over again, like you said it then.'

'I cannot.'

'You can. Say it, and say it, and I'll say yours.'

He was demonically possessed. He laughed and lit his pipe, filling the bedroom with plumes of blue smoke. She coughed but he made no apology, only beamed at her with sparkling eyes.

'I knew, you see,' he said.

'Knew?'

'When the thunder came. Do you remember the thunder?'

She nodded.

'Well then I knew. Knew how lonely you were, and courteous,

and timorous. Knew then what you needed the best. Warm home, warm hearth. And now here for ever I'll be. And now there for ever you'll be. That ring says it all. Engagement ring. Wedding ring more like. Elizabeth, you're my *wife*.'

He jerked the word with an excess of dark tenderness that made his voice go husky, and brought his face lowering down on hers for another kiss. Randomly she thought of Surtees, wondered how she had survived so long in this atmosphere of possession.

'Mr Hudson, don't. I'm only a fetish.'

'You're a what!' He laughed hugely. 'Go on, speak in your lovely strange difficult tongue. It don't flummox and frighten me no more. My . . . fetish! My heart's joy. My bible. I shall learn to read through you. All the difficult causes o' the earth will be made clear. Fetish me some more, my dear one.'

'Mr Hudson.'

'Mrs Hudson.'

'This is all wrong, impossible.'

'Ay, 'tis that, wonderful though 'ent it?'

'There's something I must tell you.'

'There's everything you must tell me. I'm a stupid chap. Not bookwise in the ways of womenfolk. Always thought a woman was hoyden at heart. Corn dolly! You've brought a bigger harvest home than ever you'd guess at.'

'I'm in love . . .'

It was all he required. She had great difficulty in keeping him from her at that moment. The word had magic properties. She struggled against his kisses.

'With somebody else.'

He scarcely heard her. His face was in her hair, when he lifted it he was pale with desire.

'Elizabeth.'

'Yes.'

'You was made for me. I read it in the Psalms. "For a thousand years in thy sight are but as yesterday when it is past, and as a watch in the night." '

'That's blasphemy.'

''Tis truth. I read it in the good book. The pages came apart under my hand. "Thou hast ascended on high, thou hast led captivity captive." There, 'tis truth, say what anyone will against it. I shall take up book-learning to prove my worth and thou,

thou shalt not be afraid for the terror by night; nor for the arrow that flieth by day, nor for the pestilence that walketh in darkness, nor for the destruction that wasteth at noonday. All nature and all nature's fears shall be but as the bull that was sent to vex thee.'

'Oh Mr Hudson, you sent it yourself.'

'Did I? Did I do so? Well happen I did so, if only to prove to thee my words was true. All horrors shall flee away even like Jonas the bull.'

'Poor Jonas.'

'Ah, 'tis poor Jonas now, but 'twas terrible Jonas then. And the hands of time himself shall be but as the bull in mine. Look!'

He went to the grandfather clock, opened the face, seized the hands.

'What time shall it be?'

'What time is it now?'

'All time, any time.'

'Let it be now the time it was yesterday.'

Triumphantly he twirled the hands in a twenty-four hour circle.

'You see? The room has not moved. You're still here, and I shall still thee an thou thee to thy face, not to thy writing in a letter. When thou art here time stands still. There. 'Tis yesterday already.'

Tears were running down her face.

'There. There, my dearest, you've had a terrible shock. I'll leave you now. But I shall return, and still return, and always you'll be lying there.'

'No Mr Hudson, I *must* talk to you.'

'Well talk on then. Say what you will and I'll prove it so or disprove it not so.'

'Mr Hudson, when I came here I was promised to another.'

'And now you find you're promised to me, like so. Well 'tis no problem to the hands of time.'

'To me it is a problem.'

'Ah yes, I can see that,' he conceded from the imperialism of his joy. 'I must remember. I shall buy thee a watch to commemorate this hour with. Wheniver thou turnest the hands, thou wilt remember.'

'Mr Hudson I shall remember all my life that you saved me . . .'

'Ah that thou will. Every day shall be a new way of

remembering.'

'... but you saved me for another. Mr Hudson I am *promised* ...'

'I'll hear no more about promises.'

'It was the greatest act of magnanimity of which a human being is capable ... To save a girl's life, and to save it for the sake of an enemy.'

'I'll have no enemies. Only friends. Come now, Elizabeth, say who 'tis, there's a dearest.'

'Mr Rex Buckley.'

'Phew, I'll scout him. Tiddn't worth a hair of your head.'

'To me he is.'

'Soft spoken chap wi' ideas. Tiddn't ideas you want my dear, it's life itself. That's my ring on your finger and you'll find it as strongly implanted there as that old ring round Jonas's nose. Girt old struggle he'd have to pull 'un off an all.'

He chuckled hoarsely in his throat.

'Mr Hudson, it's not for you to say.'

'Nor for you neither, my lady. Now you lie still awhile and let what bides, bide. Time is allus stronger than circumstances. You've done a good deed today, laying in my arms like a lamb. No point is spoiling it with false fires. Lie you still, lady, and submit.'

It was pointless trying to talk to him in this mood.

'I want you free from the house and all the fuss up there. For mark my words, when they discover you're to be the wife of Roger Hudson there will be a fuss.'

'Roger, I'll be no man's wife.'

'Is that a threat, my lady?'

'I never knew ...'

'Tut, tut, you knew well enough to be pleased to see me I warrant. First 'tis this, then 'tis that. Like all women, I surmise, you don't know the quality of your own mind. Give me another kiss.'

'No.' But the no was quickly throttled.

'No man's wife indeed.'

'It's true. If it gives you pain ... You cannot say I led you on ...'

'No? What of the letter?'

'It was written in innocence. But if you claim that that letter was the cause, I'll take the blame, truly I will. Please hear me out Mr Hudson, I hardly know what to say.'

'Say nothing, lie still.'

For she was half out of bed, distracted beyond the confines of her sick dizziness.

'If I have led you on or seemed to do so — if however innocently I have been the cause of all this, then I accept the blame and I will ...'

'Marry me!' he said triumphantly.

'Marry no man,' she answered obdurately.

This caused him dissatisfaction. He could tell she meant it.

'Elizabeth,' he said.

There was no answer. She had fallen back on the pillow. Her face was very flushed.

'No man is worth you.' He said this in a wondering undertone. 'For I believe you would and all. All for a bargain. Well, I'll have no bargaining on our day of joy. Tomorrow you may bargain. Today you're my wife.'

She submitted to his taking her hand.

'There, you see,' he added, 'you allow me favours, then withdraw them!'

She pulled her hand away, wiped her brow.

'At the moment everything I do is wrong. Don't you see, we're all trammelled up in wrong circumstances. I feel sorry for you, truly I do ...'

'Sorry!' he said. '*You* feel sorry for *me*? As though to say I be the weaker vessel. No, no, Elizabeth, the sorrow is reserved for me. Howsoever all this turns out I shall bear it better than you. If so be it you decide not to marry at all, so be it I shall bear that burden and bear it better. You've poisoned my heart with your ways and your wiles, until I almost believed it true. I felt I had you in my grasp. Well, you've slipped away. I felt you were to be mine according to the message of the Lord. Well it's not to be. But whichever way it is or is not to be, the burden now is mine, and we will see who bears the stiffest hardship without murmuring. There, those are my last words, sealed with this final kiss, which I take of thee not as down payment on my desire, which is heavy, but as ratification of what's been said. Signed and sealed by me in this room, God help me on this day, September twenty-first in the year of our Lord. Elizabeth.'

He kissed her and groped his way out of the room, leaving

her stunned at the misfortunes which she seemed to multiply around her.

A visit from Adeline proved no help. To marry her father would have been an act of injustice; to repudiate him was an act of gross injustice.

'It was his game,' she said, 'and now you've spoiled his play.'

XIII

Work without hope [says the poet] draws nectar in a sieve
And hope without an object cannot live.

At least two figures in our story are in this unhappy condition. One continues his work in a state of treadmill dreariness, the other waits and sees no end to her misfortunes.

She has left the farm, for good. The gifts have all been gathered up and placed into a drawer which has now become a coffin. She has consented to wear the ring, as a pledge to her widowed condition.

If Miss Oldcastle had practised as she threatened, she could have achieved no end nearer to her heart than this state of sterility: the fusion of I cannot with I will not.

She still takes her walks but finds no pleasure in them. Everything seems dark and shady and imprisoning. The fish are dying, the roses overblown and the birds seem like demons.

She felt herself distracted by the very places that had soothed her formerly. She felt herself transported to some high place for which she had no key, no way of unlocking the clamorous or dumb voices that counselled her in vain to go this way or that. She was indeed 'sullenly drifting', saw the fields stripped of their pomp as no more than grey lands, salt and brackish, all unstirring. Felt she was waiting for a call, but knew no call that could unlock the thoughts that were locked up in her and battered and fattened on her slowly. It was a mood of wan hope, where all man's miseries seemed present in an aspect of the mind. The free, almost picaresque lives she had been moving among thickened to demons, and took possession of her. Every move, every mood was a denial. Figures of faith were turned from her and seemed to mock her. All her appetency was in a stroke denied, rendered absurd, and cruelly ridiculous. She wrote a letter to Rex explaining her wretched state, and explaining why she could no longer think of marrying him. She was a virgin widow, awaiting only thicker and thicker duress of darkness. She saw only the ridiculousness of her state and the need to free herself of all her promises. It had been an act of hubris — to go so far into the cannon's mouth of other people's desires and grossly protuberant malevolences.

Why, she might have asked, why pierce high-fronted humour to the quick, for nothing but a dream?

Yet all around her the world *was* stirring; the mood was hers alone. The wind fell on the apple trees and upswept them, into bright clouds and tufts of sky. She saw the beauties but only saw them; could ignite no corporeal relationship with their joy in ever becoming. She had failed — the knowledge weighed on her heart. They were all, it seemed, waiting for her to become Flora, to render the earth delicious to them, and she had fallen back, shared their lassitude and dumb uncertainties. To autumn would succeed winter, to winter spring, to spring summer, then it would be autumn again. All sense of ritual had departed, and the years' seasons seemed like spokes in a wheel, where time had grown circular and would remain so until her death. She had failed the great act of transcendence and had become as one of those who await deliverance in turn. She saw no future except to grow old among sick people, sickening with their sicknesses, felt herself to have become a burden among the burdensome. Some surplus of faith in her own creative energies had led her to embrace this season as a trial, but now she was all unfitted, and felt the terrible vulnerability of life as a thing that preyed on others and itself. To return to the hospital in her present state was well-nigh an impossibility, yet she saw no option but to return, with a slackening of purpose and a failed sense of mission. Reality had triumphed over her sublime sense of unreality. Life contracted from the freedom of her being to the crabbed limitations of being a spinster. A dried-up thing, fit only to grow old with a dusty face, and eventually to wear brown stockings and perhaps carry a stick. Well, it was a fate others had had in store. That mysterious thing called age began to afflict her. She could suddenly see that there was no fixed, pastoral gap between being young and having health, and being old — being translated from one of the carriers to one of the carried. Carried — the very word reminded her of carrion. She had thought of herself as an eagle among eagles, and found, to her sickness and great lassitude that she was as a lamb among vultures. Bitter moods to which as stranger she had been able to minister, became her moods. She began to suffer from dreams of terrible hardship, felt herself to be a part of the suffering web of things. A dream of fulfilment had been unfulfilled; it was a very slight setback in the inscrutable face of the human clock but to Elizabeth as an individual it was a disaster.

She carried tears around inside her; they remained unshed. Sometimes she wished that the gate-vein of her body would burst, to release tears mixed with blood. At other times she longed for a keener, more detached vision of things which would allow her being to survive the transposition from being a free human creature into that of becoming a failed part in a complex plot — a plot not willed by anyone in particular but in which synthesis of human desires and appetites she had become a passive agent.

Meanwhile the weather continued in a dusty state of mind. There was dusty sunlight, dusty heat; there were dusty insects, like hoverflies that buzzed and bumbled in various terminal states.

One thing was solved and resolved. She could stay here no longer. Whatever Rex's plan had been — and it was a plan she had trusted — it could not have included this weird twist of the farmer's infatuation. He had probably imagined no further than life at the house itself, and trusted somehow to her bringing, by ways he had faith in, new life to the house. She had felt capable of being such a messenger — a John the Baptist, she thought grotesquely, at any rate — but now all such potential was denied her. Strange how much she had relied on the shadowy presence of Rex, and strange how his very shadowiness had been until recently the impetus behind her survival. It was love with a stranger, and love that had accumulated around his strangeness as snow will gather snow upon itself.

What had she come out of it with? She sat in her dusty attic, warmed by the friendless sunshine, totting up accounts — not for this week or next week but for life.

A word of honour paid down to a stranger never to marry. Was Mr Hudson, then, a stranger? Part of her protested against consigning him in this way. He was a friend, who had sought out her loneliness and wished to protect her. That was the trouble, it seemed — her vulnerability. Other people tended to make more of her than she herself was able. For she was not witty, was not clever, was not anything more then the sum of her moods. Such people are easy to exploit, and in a way Elizabeth had been exploited. She had waited for something to happen; it had not happened, and now she felt changed, that was all.

Useless to say she was young, that time was on her side. Time for what? Time for patience, time for conversation, time for medication, time for tea. The rituals of her returning profession afflicted her with a kind of horror. Horror partly at their sterility, horror partly at the changed perceptions that would operate on it. Until now she had considered herself as, within limits, a useful person, able not to affect great changes but able to cope. Now she felt herself unlimited but futile. She had become an individual and felt the presence of her mortality in becoming one. She would not be able to cope.

Yet part of her laughed at the accusation. Part of her would remain able to cope — that too was part of the horror. She would remain the name on a door: Doctor Elizabeth Greycliffe. Unmarried — well she had never had much hope of such an honour. She would die as she lived — a maid.

> Wheneas the rye reach to the chin,
> And chopcherry, chopcherry ripe within,
> Strawberries swimming in the cream,
> And schoolboys playing in the stream,
> Then O, then O, then O, my true love said,
> Till that time come again
> She could not live a maid.

But she could, therein lay the sadness. Miss Elizabeth Greycliffe — maid, deceased. She chuckled. They would never be able to write deceased. A maid possessed of two hearts, what was more! Till the time of her decease came round she must honour the year. Soon there would be daffodils blowing their silent bells so strenuously in the dawn of the year. There would be madrigals of lilacs and bluebells. The fruit would be green again, ripening towards autumn. And the snow would come, softer than sleep, rinsing and cleansing the mind of all its affections and infatuations.

Strange how her mind battened on Mr Hudson. Rex would cope. He had his ideals still, his proofs to search for an England that was diffusely fertile and wispily alive. He had his seashells to search for. He was a lady's man, he would find another and submit her to tests even more extravagantly strange, and she would fail or succeed, and if she succeeded, why he would marry her, and she would cease to be a maid.

But Mr Hudson would not cope. What had he called her once? Maidy. That was it. He saw her true singleness which was why he knew his love was absurd and had been carried to such absurd strengths to declare it. Maidenhood was infinite and perplexed, marriage perplexed but definite. The failure was not really so great after all. She was making the choice all along. Her mystery, such as it was, existed only as far as her singleness.

Did that then make her like Miss Oldcastle after all? Perhaps that had been the deep secret of Rex's plan; to set her sterile fertility in the context of one who was both sterile and infertile. Perhaps, indeed, she was a little mad — mad to have agreed in the first place. Then her mind went back in fondness to the little seaside, and the church that squatted like a slug against the seawet cliffs and thought of him enunciating her name to himself over and over again, and thought that that was not it. Love is a curious emotion, it leads so easily to moods of self-abnegation. When she loved him she became a maid. What did the men in Dickens say? One said WOT LARX, but another said, 'It's all a muddle.' She had never expected many larks but the muddle was infinite.

She felt her mind going drowsy. It was a little death. There would be others. It was time to make an end. She picked up her pen, addressed the letter to Mr Rex Buckley in London, and wrote.

XIV

In the library she read: 'How strange and awful is the synthesis of life and death in the gusty winds and falling leaves of an autumnal day!'

She was spending many of her last days there.

As for Hudson, he was quiet and berserk. A photograph of Elizabeth had been taken by Adeline before the episode of the bull, and he spent much time with it, admiring its proportions and finding in it all kinds of consolations for the departed one. He spoke to it, treated it tenderly as though it were a live thing. In fact he spent his time between the photograph and nocturnal visitations to the house. In the full light of the moon he would climb the fence, and walk upon the lawn in his heavy boots, crushing out juice and perfume, hearing the worms twisting and knotting with strange savagery in the thick grass, leaving it bruised with his footprints. He would watch the figures and shadows behind the curtains, guessing which one was his beloved. He knew she lived at the top of the house, and would stand gazing upward to where he hoped his darling lay, head thrown back, looking in the moonlight, with his hands stuffed in his pockets, and his body braced inside its dufflecoat, like a weird statue. The statue breathed stertorously, mingling prayers with muffled oaths. Once or twice he crunched on gravel and set the dogs barking ferociously. Someone came out from the house and quieted them, to his satisfaction, though even afterwards one of them strained and moaned almost in its sleep at the stranger's presence.

Then he would return to the farm, and at any time of the day and night would break away from his ordinary business and mourn over the photograph. He hung the cross around it, admiring the shape as it bit into the girl's image beneath it. Then

he took it into his mind that to keep an image of her in such
an exact shape was to betray his trust in what she had said. He
decided to burn the photograph. This he did one night after
a visit to the house, when he was certain he had glimpsed her
through parted curtains. He stood it in an ashtray and ignited
the lower part of her dress. He watched silently as the flame
crept upwards, but when it came to her breasts and began to
eat the soft rounded skin above her dress he found he was
emitting low groans of desire, and he snatched the card out of
the flame, dusting it into his sleeve until the fire was
extinguished. The partly consumed body loomed at him like
Joan of Arc — the lips, characteristically parted, seemed to call
to him. He kissed the face passionately and stood there awhile
sweating with bafflement. The light danced from her eyes. He
wanted to burn her totally but could not. Eventually he rekindled
the flame and watched the fire go up into her lips and hair, eating
them voraciously. At the very last moment before the flames
extinguished her she seemed to call to him.

Then once again up the track to the house. Perhaps she still
required him. Mr Hudson's obstinate, unyielding nature was
hard to contact, but once contacted was almost irresistible in
its force. It was impossible for him to feel that he had lost her.
She was waiting for him, in need, it was still up to him to break
down the bounds of her restraint and make her acknowledge
him. He had this slow-working message in his brain like an
animal.

There was the question of the clothes. At first he thought of
burying these too, like the photograph; then gradually another
obsession took him over. He would keep them until they were
old and rotten, keep them until the moth and rust corrupted
them, until they gaped at him with a sense of time gone by.
They were her trousseau: very well, they would remain her
trousseau until the end of his time on earth. When he died they
would go with him into the coffin. He willed it so: the contents
of his top drawer to be put into the coffin with him on his decease.
There he would hug them through eternity. They would drape
his skeleton. Elizabeth — there! He continued to name her. In
some way or other he would possess her, even unto the fever
of his skeleton. His bones would reek through her cloth.

He essayed another letter. It was a failure. Why, he could
not tell, but he screwed it up and threw it away. It lacked passion.

The words did not do what they ought — they ought to burn like fire. He wished he could simply write 'Come!' and that she would come. He would gladly be her servant if he could so order and ordain it. He would drink pismire gladly if it would bring her to him.

He was utterly wounded by her rejection. Not having much imagination he could not see *why* she had rejected him. He wanted her sufficiently for two people — that was surely enough. Besides, she was beauteous and strange, like the moon. He wanted to net her, like those people who threw nets into a pond when the moon was at its full. All he found were ripples of the magnitude of his desire spoiling the perfection of her figure. He muddled her with want.

'Oh my Elizabeth,' he groaned into his duffel-coat at nights, striding the uplands or standing at the house. 'Oh my darling, come down to me.'

He sent her the cross. It was not returned. That was a good sign, surely! He was like a child that could not understand its rejection. If you wanted something badly enough it would come to you. She should be like his animals. They obeyed his desires. Among the animals he was heavy and sturdy as earth itself. When a cow broke free at milking-time, he knew how to bring her back within the rest of the herd. When a bull grew restive he had the strength in his forearm to bring it to its knees. He loved trials of strength. Even with his men he would sometimes indulge in elbow wrestling. Always he won, not simply because they knew he would be offended if he lost. And now he could not understand the failure of his will. He had lost his shaping power. He could not wrestle her into the shelter of his warmth. It baffled him. For he knew he was warm and reliable. He knew he could provide for her. And yet she said no — unless to accept the cross meant yes. He construed it to mean yes, whatever the circumstances. It was natural that she had not said yes at first. Women did not like to do so. They were not like men. They had strange ways of their own. It would not be decent for her to succumb without a struggle. He must continue to ply her until she said yes properly.

In such ways did his mind run on, and always with the slow working certainty that he was in the right and she was in the wrong. At times he felt this so distinctly as almost to triumph over her. She *must* see things his way and eventually would. At other times he knew he was fighting, for the first time in life, a stronger will than his own, and felt blind and bleared with rage that things were not working out. Let her only come to him.

She did not come. The days at the house were very limited in number now. She had to let Miss Odlcastle know that she was leaving — a difficult problem, for the old lady had come to rely on her in her grumpy fashion. The other servants were indifferent. They regarded her as a fortune hunter and would laugh thoroughly when she left without her fortune. Well, let them. Her face was her fortune, she told herself, though without much conviction, for when she studied it in the mirror it told a different story, being wan and desolate. A maid in autumn, that was she. 'And young men glittering and sparkling angels, and maids strange seraphic pieces of life and beauty' — no seraph she, for sure, either to herself or to others. If he could see her now: but already the line dividing Rex from Mr Hudson was melting and blurring under the pressure of her vow, and who ever saw her would see in her nothing except a pale, firmset, rather off-putting young lady with gracious but determined dark brows, and an attitude, assumed at first, but later to become habitual, that between life and work and the world there were very few divisions. The air of high comedy and latent romance that had attracted Mr Buckley had disappeared. Even Surtees noticed it, and kept his distance both physically and verbally. She was, in a way, dying, and the death was sad to contemplate even if you were an indifferent bystander, whose ideas harped on all the wrong strings.

She had come to the house like a Renaissance girl, quick to play games, full of improvisational spirit, with a sense of farce lurking exuberantly in the wings of her destiny; she was leaving like a Victorian heroine, defeated in some essential gaiety of spirit, even if her beauty was unbowed.

That it should be up to her to arrange the scenes she had inhabited! She longed for some *deus ex machina* to tumble people's emotions into a jigsaw of possibilities where none were hurt but all were affected.

The idea of Mr Hudson played extensively on her conscience. Looking out of the window late at night, she had seen him standing amid the stars, waiting for the insoluble knot to loosen. She knew he wanted her to rush to him in her nighdress, hair streaming, to beg for his protection. If only Rex had come to her like that. But he would not. He was waiting for her to achieve the miracle which her passiveness was unable to figure forth. Another woman for Mr Hudson! The impossible idea made her lips writhe in laughter even as she choked on a sob. He was so obdurate, waiting there to catch her as she crawled through the rigging of this tempestuous barque, she bearing only one name on the mind. Or if only there was a Mr Rochester to unblind her from her infatuation.

Perhaps it was not Miss Oldcastle who was mad. Perhaps lurking in the depths of the house there was another woman, unnamed and unseen, who was awaiting some magic touch of liberation. Perhaps the house was waiting to spring into secret life and laughter if she could find the right spring to press.

She became obsessed with the idea, and unconsciously went around everywhere, touching the furniture and the panels, hoping for a click and a whirr. Anything, even if it was only a laundry bill like in Jane Austen, would have helped to clarify her mind. If the other servants saw her, and they did sometimes, it would only solidify the idea they already had of her in their heads.

How vaulted, peculiar and hollow the house was! Not only the gallery, the whole building from its wainscotting to its high panelled chambers was one great echo-chamber. No wonder the wind inhabited it so peculiarly. Scarcely a day passed without some new music being made in the different stresses of the beams. It was very much like being at sea. Or like a theatre, when nobody was there except for a few stagehands. A deserted theatre, which somehow she had once imagined would be flooded with light and music.

Meanwhile she had a sick woman to cope with — sick and intractable. Miss Oldcastle's moods did not get any easier. Though there had been no repetition of the scene with the axe, and though that scene had faded in Elizabeth's mind as she grew more familiar with the mental landscape she was living in, Miss Oldcastle's words continued to cut like axes. She seemed to have no idea that anybody existed except for herself. The people — servants, family — she summoned up were all extensions of her own warped being, all sick like her, all bent on one thing, self.

'They rob me at night', she once confided, with tears sparkling dangerously on her lower lashes.

That was how Elizabeth came to be doing night-duty. It was

another twist of her employer's insanity — that she should be sitting up all night, waiting for an invader.

She sat in the gallery, with a candle that flaked and fluttered and turned blue as the ghosts of the wind outside tugged at it. Gradually the house settled itself to sleep around her, with much ado of creaking as though tossing and turning inside a gigantic whalebone corset.

Miss Oldcastle had retired to her room; there was no-one about.

At about one o'clock she went downstairs to the kitchen to make some coffee. The kitchen was a huge room with stone inlays; it looked supernaturally bright. There was a red chintz tablecloth on the pine planked table, and a big clock that ticked solemnly to itself — a clock with a white staring face. Elizabeth had met the cook, a big cheerful woman, but there was, at this hour, no sign of her. The fire was low in the range but warm enough to boil water, and Elizabeth had run the water into a big glossy steel kettle, and set it to boil.

It took a long time. Not even the preliminary hum was audible. The clock ticked hypnotically, and the occasional displacement of ash in the grate only added to the drowsy atmosphere. Elizabeth felt herself sinking into sleep. She was sitting in a big Windsor chair with her back to the window. She heard the wind steaming through tunnels of trees, and felt sleep pressing her eyelids down like a huge healing hand. It was irresistible, though she tried to resist — started, sank, sank, started and finally sank.

The hiss of the kettle boiling over awoke her from a dream about anaesthetic surgery: someone was bunging her face full of wadding to stop it bleeding. She struggled blindly for a moment until she recognized the noise of the kettle and realized where she was. The lid of the kettle was bob-bobbing under pressure of steam, and spits of steam were hissing on the black-leaded range. Still half asleep she tried to stand, but felt herself to be pinned in the chair. Bells were ringing inside her head. She had a great sense of danger, even though there was nothing apparently wrong. Could it be Miss Oldcastle? Without lifting the kettle from the hob she went out of the kitchen, up the great gaunt staircase to the gallery. It was as usual full of sound, but there was nothing special in the sounds. She tried Miss Oldcastle's door. It was not locked and opened easily. No sound from within. She paced further in. There was a stifled snore. She bent down to look. Her employer was apparently sound asleep, and yet . . . She backed away, irresolute. A cackle of laughter decided her. She fetched the candle from the gallery. It was worn and wasted away yet still shed light. With one hand shading the light and feeling like Florence Nightingale, she re-entered the room, supernaturally sensitive to the way raindrops plucked and pecked on the sill outside. There she found Miss Oldcastle with eyes wide open, watching her. Elizabeth asked her a question. There was no answer.

'You see,' said Miss Oldcastle triumphantly, 'they all do it. Even you. And I trusted you, Greycliffe. Well I trust you no longer. You're sacked.'

'Miss Oldcastle, I . . .'

'You're sacked. No references. I knew you were bad.'

There seemed no point in arguing. In one way it saved the trouble of further explanations. But it was distressing to have to go in such a way.

'Miss Oldcastle, I . . .'

'You're a thief. Worse than the others put together. At the deadest time of night. Return to your duties at once. *At once!* Do you hear?'

'I came to see if you were all right.'

'You came to see if I was dead. Well I ain't. Feel this wrist.'

Elizabeth felt it.

'Feel the blood in it? Blood that is life. Pumping away. I ain't dying to please no-one except myself.'

'No, Miss Oldcastle.'

'Blame me if I do.'

There was nothing to be said, and nothing to be done, except to return to her lonely vigil. She went downstairs again to the kitchen, and made coffee in a big brown earthenware jug. There was a bottle of gold-topped thick cream milk in the larder and she took some, feeling herself resolved by accident.

The coffee was warming and helped to reassure her jangled nerves. At least she could leave with a good conscience. In spite of the hour she found herself laughing. A strange holiday, to end up getting the sack. The phrase was brutal and brief. She had proved unsatisfactory and the axe had come for her head. Like Lady Jane Grey!

Rain was still chipping away outside. She drew the big

curtains and looked out on the wet blackness. It was so immense, the out-there, it terrified her with its lack of form, its wet incompleteness. Form was so necessary to life. Here in the great house she had lost her independence, and lost a sense of the little niggling essential details out of which life made up its shape. Without realising it she had been drawn into the grasp of a great obsession which was itself a kind of form. It had made her gasp and stretch her eyes like the little boy who was so fond of telling lies, but it had failed to encompass her.

Dawn found her still in the kitchen, white and wan but composed and sure-footed. Today or tomorrow she would leave.

XV

'Then I got the sack.'
'The *sack*?'
'Exactly as I tell you. That's why I left.'
'Oh *Lizzie*.'
'Why do you say that?'
'And you so much in control. Nobody will ever sack you.'
'Well they just have.'
'And not a word from Rex?'
'I had a letter. It didn't help much.'
'I never had a word from him. I told you. He's miles in advance of me.'
'So much that he disappears in the distance?'
'So it seems.'
'It was a strange experience.'
'Pleasurable.'
'Not really, no I couldn't say that. It did things to me that I shan't forget.'
'Oh, you will forget. It sounds like a dream.'
'Well, it was in a way. Nigel, I made a contract.'
'What sort of contract?'
'A very strange one. I said I would never marry.'
'Oh you ... To yourself?'
'No, to a man.'
'Another man?'
'Yes.'
'Lizzie, your life's suddenly become full of men.'
'Well, it did. Now it's become very empty of them again.'
'Aren't you curious?'
'No, I don't think so. I think you're the curious one.'
'Look at the sea!'

'Yes, it's lovely. Would you like a swim?'
'No, it'll be too cold.'
'Yes.'
'Lizzie, you are changed somehow. Less, less summery.'
'Yes.'
'And more compliant. Why do you keep saying yes?'
'It was my job. I had to comply.'
'You never were very compliant before.'
'Wasn't I?'
'No, you've lost something.'
'I feel as though I've lost everything. It was a kind of game, I expect. And I lost.'
'Liz.'
'Yes.'
'I'm glad you're back.'
'So am I. So am I Nigel, I'm very glad.'
'Wiser and better, eh?'
'No, I feel very foolish.'
'Better safe than sorry.'
'There was so much that could have been done, that should have been said.'
'You'll remember it all eventually.'
'When it's too late.'
'Perhaps.'
'It's all in a month's experience.'
'A month! It feels like a lifetime. Do you remember how we sat here, and you said you knew a man? And how we both crippled ourselves on those rocks? Nigel, let's take a walk.'
'We've only just sat down.'
'Let's take another walk. Beside the sea. Listening to its doings.'

> 'It keeps eternal whisperings around —
> Desolate shores, and with its mighty swell —
> Gluts twice ten thousand Caverns —
> Oh ye! whose ears are dinn'd with uproar rude
> Or fed too much cloying melody —
> Sit ye near some old Cavern's Mouth and brood —
> Until ye start, as if the sea nymphs quir'd!'